GW01424312

Acknowledgements

A special thank you to Nicola Anne Johns, Artist/poet, for all artistry and design work of the cover, interior pages and poetry works.

www.nicolajohnsartist.com

The Owlsden Witches

Dance of Death

By

Leon McAvoy

Leon McAvoy is committed to publishing works of quality and integrity. In that spirit we are proud to offer to our readers, The Owlsden Witches, Dance of death© a story inspired by true events. Subsequently some individual names and place names have been changed to protect individuals and communities.

A CIP catalogue record for this title is available from the British Library.

ISBN 978-1-5272-7094-7 (Paperback)

www.LGMMcAvoy.com

First Published (2020)

LGM McAvoy Ltd C/N 12479450

To MARGARET
HOPE YOU ENJOY
LOTS OF LOVE
Ronn x

45/300

In the Beginning

Two hundred and fifty million years ago the earth a beautiful blue gem turned silently, majestically against the backdrop of a black velvet universe. Back then the earth looked much different than it does today. The ocean was one vast expanse of beautiful blue liquid of differing shades. It contained and bound within its ring of water one huge continent of land. It would take many years of volcanic and seismic disruption to violently rip apart this mass of rock and form the many countries that we have on this day come to know as, our earth.

Then, out from where we know not, comes a ball of flame, from one of the far flung dark and cold corners of this cathedral like universe, it roars this torch of light, directly toward the gently turning aqua planet. This sphere of fire heading toward the very epicentre of this water locked land.

It briefly disappears from their view but then a pin prick flash of light tells them of its sudden and violent Impact within this land, an area that later becomes known as England and a place that comes to be known as Owlsden.

The St Valentine Day's Massacre

Friday 14th February 2020 8:37am, London

Dr Oliver James Williams a physician and specialist at the Great Ormond Street Hospital London is making his way towards the apple market of Covent Garden. For those who did not know The Great Ormond Street hospital is a children's hospital specialising in the treatment and care of sick children and has become renowned around the world for the wonderful work that it does for our little ones.

Oliver is on the clock for he must find a journal, ornate in its design and nature, something that speaks of the character of his only child Emily. For some years now Oliver had observed how Emily would scribble down her inner most thoughts on all and any scraps of paper and bundle these up into a scruffy folder that had become decidedly tatty. *No! she now needs a journal, book of sorts that these most treasured of thoughts could for once reside and be at peace. Nice paper within and perhaps a good pen to boot.* Whilst he was at it, he would look for a piece of jewellery for his wife Samantha, something quirky something antique, unique, *she would like that,* he thinks. He and Samantha had met at university, he was studying medicine and she veterinary and had fell in love immediately and up until recently they had not been apart for more than a few days at a time, but then he took this position at the Great Ormond.

It was a career choice, something they had sat and discussed long into the night and both agreed that despite it coming between them, it was the right thing to do and they were strong enough in their relationship for it not to have a detrimental effect, and besides, he thought, *absence makes the heart grow fonder* they say, but he was missing his girls anyway.

These next two weekends were important, special, the second weekend was Emily's birthday, her eighteenth, *'wow!' it seemed like yesterday,* him racing to the hospital in Bury St Edmunds late into the evening on that Friday night, Samantha in the back of the car shouting at him between moans to *'be careful'* in case they came across someone taking their dog for a late night walk along the lanes. She had always been thoughtful like that; *wow! was 2002 really eighteen years ago?* he thought. Emily was born that night, a typical Picarian, just like her mother caring and sensitive and the fact that he wasn't going to be home for her birthday, the weekend after next was tearing him up, but what could he do? *works, work.* That's why he had to make this weekend extra special.

Oliver had decided to walk from the hospital to Covent Garden instead of taking a cab, the Stroll would help him to clear his head and besides, he'd enjoy the exercise. Oliver was and had never been known for one who spent hours in a gym or particularly renowned as a sportsman but then he had been blessed with good genes and his five-foot eight stature was lean considering his diet and he did on occasion take himself for a run around the country lanes of that small hamlet in which they lived, which as it happened was not as tranquil as it sounded, despite the county of Suffolk being renowned for its flatness and hence great arable land this one small corner of Suffolk ramped up to over four hundred feet above sea level and thus contained some unusually steep hills that would just as dramatically drop into winding valleys with picturesque streams below.

Suddenly becoming aware of his surroundings Oliver was about to say to himself that it obviously had everything to do with it being a Valentines weekend that the streets were so busy but then he reminded himself that *this is London and it's always busy,* regardless of any holiday and about a million miles away from that tiny hamlet in that deepest darkest part of Suffolk County that they had come to call 'home.' *But how weird that we have become all too eager to celebrate anything at the drop of a hat,* but hey he was no different, he was about to do the same at home with his girls, and he couldn't wait, and again Oliver was reminded of just how much he was missing them and home.

So, here was the plan, he'd get to the stall that sold the handmade journals, it would probably take a while to choose one, but it was important to get this right, but having done so perhaps he would get some breakfast; he'd worked late into the previous night due to meetings concerning developments about a virus that was coming out of China and the implications for them at the hospital and thus he hadn't the time to get anything to eat from the canteen.

He would need to be dusted and done, get back to his digs, pick up his bag he packed the day before and be at Liverpool Street Station for two o'clock to get the train to Bury St Edmunds, stopping at Ipswich on the way, scheduled to arrive at Bury at three fifty-five, hopefully?

It was a journey Oliver had taken many times over the last six months since taking the position at Great Ormond Street, and to be fair it wasn't a bad journey and generally on time, and Bury was a great little station and if Samantha got the timing just right, she was able to pull up directly outside and he would just hop in and it was then only a short thirty-minute drive of ten miles to home sweet home.

As Oliver reached the stall, he was greeted by a lady in her late forties who had a lovely smiley Face, a face that was approachable, open, friendly, "hi is there anything particular that you're looking for" she asked, "well it's for my Daughter, her eighteenth, she loves to write," said Oliver, "well, there's lots, and these here are my latest creations," she said pointing at one end of the stall. Oliver had intuitively guessed that he was talking to the creator of these wonderful journals before she even spoke, there was just something about her whole persona that spoke volumes, "thank you" said Oliver, "I'll let you know when I've found it" and the lady stepped away with another smile that left Oliver feeling unpressured.

He scans the rows of journals, picks one and takes it down from its bracket, it wasn't 'the one' he was looking for, he knew that, he wanted to just check the feel of the book, the quality.

The book was surprisingly heavy, substantial, he could feel the resistance and stiffness in the spine as he opened it and was instantly met with the smell of fresh new paper which took him back a little, he had not expected the paper within to be handmade as well, but it was, and he could clearly see flecks and grains within the paper and it was slightly rough to touch, *what a wonderful experience writing will be, Emily will just love it, now to find the right one.*

Oliver was halfway down the stall scanning from top to bottom when from the corner of his eye a journal at the very end seemed to just jump out at him. Oliver took three long strides passing all and stood and looked at *that* book, 'the one,' he knew it before he reached up and gently took it down. It was just a little smaller than A4, a good size to fit into a bag and to be carried, it was as thick and heavy as the previous one had been, but it was the colour and the design, beautiful blue and turquoise swirls brought forth a subtle but instantly recognisable image of the earth.

Oliver didn't open the journal; he could see from the edge that the paper within was the same and he wanted to keep it pristine for when Emily opened it. Oliver spun on his heels and was greeted by the smiley lady again and without him saying anything the lady greets him with, "good choice," she is going to love it," taking it from Oliver the lady wrapped it in a sheet of crepe paper of a similar colour, Oliver pays by card and slipped the wrapped journal into the main compartment of his ruck sack and his wallet back into its front pocket, he thanks the lady and in return got another wonderful sunshiny smile that makes her eyes light up, *that was a pleasure*, he thinks as he walks away.

Right, now for Samantha's present, he knew he wanted to buy her a ring, and in silver, she wouldn't wear gold, not even her wedding ring was gold and this preference was something that Emily seemed to have adopted as well, so he knew what metal it was to be, and perhaps amber? Samantha loved amber, she felt it was warm, and Oliver couldn't help but feel that this suited his wife's personality perfectly.

Not very far along Oliver comes to a stall selling what was advertised as antique jewellery and this time he was met by a gentleman who was wrapped up against the weather, thick heavy coat, fingerless mitts, scarf and a flat cap, "looking for anything particular governor," he said as Oliver approached, "well I think it's to be a ring, silver with an amber stone, if you have anything like that please," says Oliver, the man looks at Oliver quizzical whilst stroking his goatee beard, "well this just maybe your lucky day Sir," he says, turning and moving to one end of his stall, "I've just had some Baltic Amber come in, take a butcher's at that," he said, picking up a pad of silver rings with amber stones within, Oliver could not help but think the man's cockney act was just that, an act for the tourists, however he did have a very nice-looking collection of rings.

From the pad, one instantly stands out, it had ornate carvings around were the silver met and held the stone, the amber was oval and of a wonderful honey colour with some dark flecks through it, "you said 'Baltic Amber,' what's that?" said Oliver, "Amber that's from the Baltics," said the man and Oliver felt he deserved that, "did I mention I was looking for something antique," said Oliver. "forty-four million years antique enough for you?" said the man. The deal was done, and the ring placed in a box, Oliver pays and as he walks away comes a chorus of, "another happy customer ladies and gents, antique rings, try and buy." *Now*, thought Oliver, *I could do with a coffee and perhaps one of those Danish, lots of fruit and cinnamon, nice.*

Oliver finds a coffee shop, looks at his watch, 10:42am, there was plenty of time so on this occasion he decided not to get a takeaway, he did that all too often of late particularly at work, it was always, '*I'll just grab a quick one,*' but not today, no, he was going to Sit at a table for a while and enjoy a good coffee, and a Danish, relax and watch the world go by. Despite the amount of people Oliver finds a table in the food hall, gets served and as he waits, he checks his watch yet again. Both coffee and Danish were good, and he feels himself heave a big sigh, he was beginning to unwind; the overhead glass ceiling was allowing a nice amount of natural light in despite it being a rather dullish day, and he watches grey clouds float by as he takes in the string quartet playing in the corner, something classical and it makes for quite a relaxed environment.

He removed his glasses and rubbed his eyes and massaged the bridge of his nose and his thoughts turned to the coming weekend and all the good things to come, good food, *warm bed, his bed, with his gorgeous wife in it, perhaps a glass or two of nice wine by the fire and Emily, ahhh yes, Emily's face when she opens her present.* Just then an expression comes over Oliver's face, he'd had an idea that had obviously pleased him, he dived into his bag and pulled out the journal, he carefully unwraps this and oh so gently folds back the front cover trying hard not to stress the spine, there was a slight crack and he winces, he fumbles in his jacket pocket and finds one of the many pens he carries, it was a job thing, and he pauses in thought before he bursts into a flurry of writing, Oliver was particularly proud of the fact that he bucked the modern myth that all Doctors had illegible handwriting, his in fact was not just legible, it was positively elegant. Samantha had liked that about him from the very get go, that he was able to produce something so beautiful from his strong manly hands.

His thoughts turned to when they first started dating when they were both in university, weekend nights spent in each other's rooms laying on the bed naked having just made love, drinking cheap wine and discussing their future. It was a for gone conclusion that they would marry but it was all the other stuff, where they would live? what type of house would they live in? and children, yes there would be children, it didn't matter whether boys or girls but rather how many? and they discussed names and for Samantha, she wanted Emily if a girl and George if a boy, Oliver didn't mind he just loved the idea of having a family.

There came a time not long after they were married when they had the inevitable conversation as to why Sam had not fallen, and it was agreed to take tests and by this stage it really didn't come to much of a surprise when their doctor informed them that without assistance it was unlikely Sam would fall naturally. The following weeks were filled with pain and lots of soul searching, did they go down that route of IVF treatment with the uncertainty that it wasn't guaranteed, and for how long? what if this went on for years and then have to give up because it just wasn't happening, and time was of a consideration, Samantha was five years older than Oliver, not that it had ever mattered, until now, whether Samantha liked it or not her biological clock was ticking, and now in her mid-thirties it was risky for all concerned. However, in early 2001 they began the treatment and having been told repeatedly by Doctors that, "it's not always successful first time around," Sam fell, and it was announced in June of that year that Samantha was in fact very much pregnant and that the child was a girl and on February 22nd, 2002 at 10:22pm Emily came kicking and screaming into this world to two doting parents.

As Emily grew and became old enough to understand, Oliver and Samantha told her of the struggle that they had in conceiving her and in part this had led them to agreeing not to try and have any more children and so Emily grew up an only child, not that she minded.

Emily had grown a wonderful mass of deep red curly hair and it became a standing joke within the family during these discussions that perhaps there had been a mix up at the hospital and in fact Emily wasn't theirs after all, as neither Oliver nor Samantha could remember any family members on either side that had such strikingly beautiful red hair.

Oliver finishes what he was writing in the front of the journal, sits back and reads to himself the Sentiments, he blows on to the ink until he's sure its dry and carefully replaces the cover and re wraps the journal and puts it back into his ruck sack. Oliver checks his watch it was 11:57 and although he has plenty of time decides to make a move, if there was one thing he hated, it was to be placed under pressure because he was running late. Oliver wiped his mouth with a napkin stands, grabs his ruck sack pushes his chair back under the table and heads for the stairs.

As Oliver reached the first landing of the stairs, he has to go around a man seemingly just Standing there and staring down into the food hall, *he must be lost*, thought Oliver.

Oliver strolls along the upper gallery and turns the corner, it had been a good morning, he may even do some paperwork on the train up, and thus *truly put his mind to rest this weekend* he thinks, **BOOOOOM**, came the noise that literally rocked the building, the noise had been so loud and violent it shook Oliver to his core, his hearing had been affected too, he hadn't gone completely deaf, but his hearing had become muffled but not so much as to not be able to hear glass shattering and falling from height. A large plume of smoke was now coming up from the food hall where he had been moments ago, there was a moment of silence and then came the first of those horrifying screams, screams that no human wants to hear, he had experienced people in pain and the noises they made, and it never got any easier, a human afraid and in pain is somewhat primeval, scary, gut wrenching, and these screams now grow in numbers and intensity. Oliver turned unsteady on his heals and headed back toward an ever-enveloping cloud of smoke and debris falling from the ceiling. He reached the top of the stairs, all the time saying to himself, *what on earth has gone wrong*, and although he had never been in combat, the smell of cordite and burning flesh combined with a scene of utter carnage and devastation immediately told him that this had been a terrorist attack.

Oliver had to force his legs to move and once he had, his training kicked in, he covered the stairs quickly but taking care and attention as everything was covered in glass, all the time he was scanning the food hall, what were the estimated number of casualties? where was the greatest numbers within the hall? who was clearly still conscious and thus still alive and who was lying still?

Oliver wouldn't bother reaching for his phone he knew enough people would be doing that, right now, he needed to focus on the injured and dying. At the bottom of the stairs, Oliver came to the first victim, a teenage girl, she must have been heading for the stairs, with one hand he felt for a pulse in her neck and the other Oliver pushed back her hair to assess her injury's, two things struck Oliver simultaneously, her heart had stopped which would ordinarily launch Oliver into CPR mode however, there was so little bone and tissue left in her face that it would be impossible to find an airway, if in theatre there was always something that could be done, but here, on a cold stone floor of a food hall, it was never going to happen. As much as it hurt and cut into Oliver, he had to leave her, "MOVE ON!" he screamed at himself inside his head and his training again took over. To the next and an elderly gentleman who had sustained leg laceration and although he was bleeding profusely Olive knew he would be ok, Oliver instructed his wife who had been sitting beside him and had not a scratch on her, to firmly press napkins to the wounds and to keep him awake, there was no time for bedside manner here.

On standing Oliver noticed a young woman knelt beside someone, she looked as if she knew what she was doing and from beneath her winter coat Oliver caught a glimpse of a light blue tunic, their eyes connected, and Oliver said to her, "Dr Oliver Williams G/O, where are you from?" the young women answered back, "St Bart's," "what's happening there?" said Oliver referring to the victim before her, the nurse looked at Oliver and shook her head from side to side. "Ok" Oliver said "can you assist me now please nurse" the look on the young nurses was almost that of relief.

The two of them moved from victim to victim as quickly and methodically as they could, the whole time the situation becoming worst by the minute, for the amount of blood on the stone floor creating a condition similar to watching a complete novice on an ice-skating rink, that and large sheets of glass still falling from the ceiling and crashing all about them.

Both Oliver and the nurse were now covered from foot to knee, hand to elbow in people's blood but despite this they pushed on. A local shop keeper came over and gave them their first aid kit and Oliver could not but help think how grossly inadequate this was, but he was also incredibly grateful at the same time.

They broke open pressure bandages and applied, the death toll was already into double figures and he just did not want to count anymore, *push on, push on* Oliver kept saying to himself, that and "where is the help, where's the Paramedics?" out loud. What had already seemed like an age was realistically just moments and he knew it, soon help would come, *push on, push on.*

Just then two-armed Police Offices came jogging into the scene and Oliver felt a slight sense of relief, but of course, they weren't here to help him with the victims, and they set about trying to form a cordon but at least Oliver now knew that the outside world had been informed and it was now only a matter of minutes before they had backup, *push on,* Sure enough no sooner that he had said this to himself did the first Paramedics arrive and Oliver made himself known and began to direct the teams to areas and victims of immediate concern. Soon there were more first responders than needed and those surplus to requirements were given the task of the coordinated ferrying of the dying and injured to several different hospitals in the immediate vicinity as the major incident response plan kicked into full swing.

Oliver lost sight of the young nurse that had helped him, and he felt sorry he hadn't had the chance to say 'thank you' to her. His role had now become that of coordination as things were taken out of his hands, hands that at this point were still covered in blood. Just then from out of the crowded but coordinated chaos came a small entourage of Police Officers, the most senior in the centre flanked by armed Officers and several others all looking very stern and official and they were heading directly for him, he was shattered, physically, mentally and emotionally and wasn't sure he needed to speak to anyone at this point. The senior Police officer reached him and put out his hand to shake, Oliver raised his to show their condition and the Officer slightly shocked obviously withdrew the gesture. "Jack Spinner, assistant Commissioner Met and you are?" "Dr Oliver Williams G/O Sir," "very good Williams, I understand you were the first on scene?" "yes, Sir I was," "very good, may I ask that you provide a statement to one of my officers whilst it's all still fresh" "well I don't think there's much chance of it disappearing any time soon Sir, but yes of course, I can," "very good Williams," the Commissioner go's to leave stops and turns back, "oh and by the way Williams, your conduct here today has been nothing short of exemplary, heroic even, we and the people of London owe, **BOOOOOM**.

Samantha had organised her week so she could finish around lunch time, get to the shops and buy some nice food wine and picky bits and be home to shower and back out in good time to pick Oliver up from the station. She only had two appointments that morning, routine examinations for one of the local racing stables in Newmarket. After qualifying Samantha had gone to a local veterinarian and cut her teeth on her fair share of problems with, dogs, cats, hamsters, lizards, llamas and camels, yes really, 'camels', its Suffolk. But after serving her time she turned to specialising in equine medicine, it made perfect sense, here was the centre of the universe as far as horse racing was concerned with some of the largest studs and stables to be found anywhere, owned by some of the richest families in the horse racing world, why wouldn't you? It had proven to be a sensible move and very lucrative to, and over time she had become a very tried tested and trusted vet, and that was quite a feat with some of her clients, considering she was a woman, but Samantha didn't make this assumption from any bitter, feministic point of view, she truly understood and knew that she was working in what was still very much a male domain, even in this day and age.

Samantha put the shopping away, she'd cleaned house earlier that week not that it needed much as for the last few months she had practically been living on her own what with Oliver in London and Emily 'living in' at Thrashams. It had been Emily's choice to board at the private school in north Norfolk and from the very get go she loved it and thrived to the point that on occasion she wouldn't come home at weekends preferring to spend time on the beautiful north Norfolk coast or the Broads which was tough at times on Samantha as she would feel quite lonely, but hey that's Emily, true picarian she just loved the water and always did. One of the top swimmers at Thrashams, swam county and even her tutor commented that she could if she wanted, possibly make Olympic trials if it wasn't for Emily's true love, that of animals.

At first when Emily said at a young age that she wanted to be a vet Samantha just thought she was just following mummy having spent quite a bit of time by her side as she tended to many a horsey problem, but as time went on Samantha could see that Emily was truly smitten by the work and did everything she could to encourage her, not that she had to try too hard, Samantha harked back to a time they found an injured Gannet on a beach when on a family holiday in Scotland, Emily, then still quite young insisted they come to the rescue, and the poor creature not realising they were trying to help put up quite a fight but after an hour or more Emily had managed to get her jacket around the bird, the sleeves acting as restraints, then spent hours driving around Scotland trying to find someone who was prepared to take the bird in and when we finally did Emily was so pleased with herself, handing over the bird to the rescue centre the lady said to Emily "is the bird wild," "oh yes" said Emily "he's positively furious".

Emily was now in her last few months at Thrashams, she had made many friends and quite easily, she was everybody's friend and she had loved her time there and would be sorry to leave, but leave she must, to get the qualifications needed to be a vet. Emily could have gone anywhere; such were her grades and for a time it seemed she would be heading for the Royal Veterinary College London but then decided against it, purely as she felt she just wouldn't cope with being in such close proximity to so many people, so the University of Cambridge it was and the veterinary Medicine MB course it was to be, and of course that meant she wouldn't be a million miles away from mum, and her bed, and the washing machine, and the fridge, and Mr Darcy.

Samantha showered and threw on some jeans, grabs her keys and pats Mr Darcy, the family cat on the head whilst saying, "just off to get daddy, back soon," she wasn't the only person to speak to their pets she knew, closes the kitchen door and jumps into her Range Rover, Samantha had not a problem with driving such a large car, what with all the stuff going on about global warming and the climate crises, which she fully understood and supported but in her line of work she genuinely needed something like this, she spent more time in fields than on the road and in fact she would often query her need for road tax at all.

Samantha pulled out of the drive of Willow Cottage, home for the last twenty years or so, a lovely old rickety cottage that over the years had been reformed and extended extensively, in fact it was said that five hundred years ago it was originally the courthouse for the region and the very place the witch catcher general Mathew Hopkins had tried, tortured and executed several supposed local witches. When her and Oliver were told this by the then owner a Mr Broomfield the day they came to view they had looked at each other smiled and said, "cool."

Samantha always took the back roads out of Owlsden to Bury, the main Haverhill to Bury St Edmunds road *was* quicker and because of that also dangerous and hey she liked the country lanes, you would always encounter lots of wildlife, deer, lots of deer, she recalled seeing four albino deer together one time in a nearby field, something quite rare, and owls, there were more owls here than she had ever seen, she had given up counting, it wasn't even funny, you couldn't go out night or day without spotting at least one. She had plenty of time, the train wasn't due in until 15:55 so she would just poodle along. Samantha arrive at the station at around 15:45 and was happy to just pull over and wait, you could wait outside the station to pick up so long as you didn't leave your car. Samantha turned on radio two to listen to some music whilst she waited. She had tried to call Oliver just to let him know she was there, but there had been no response, which was par for the course, either he was going under bridges or more likely his phone was playing up again, it had started to do that ever since his contract had expired, she resorted to leaving a text. 16:05 and still no sign of Oliver, Samantha thought, *bloody train is late again,* ok what she'll do, although it was a bit risky, was lock the car, leave it where it was run into the station, the ticket office was just there on the right and quickly ask if his train had been delayed. The song on the radio was cut short and the presenter announced, "apologies, but we are going direct to our newsroom for some breaking news", Samantha cut the ignition and the car died, she jumped out and ran around the back of the car and into the station, "excuse me, has the 15:55 from Liverpool Street come in or has it been delayed" she asked of the man in the kiosk, he looked up "yes Madam, been and gone" "ok thanks" she said, heading back to the car she was relieved to see she hadn't got a ticket, "damn it" she said aloud, "he's gone and missed the bloody train again". There was nothing for it she would have to head home and see if she could contact him or wait until he contacted her to say what train he'd be on, but one thing for sure there was no point in waiting, the next train was more than an hour away, "oh well," Samantha thought.

On the leisurely drive back, Samantha gets a call from Emily, "Hi Mum," "Hi darling," "have you got dad yet?" "no darling, he's missed the train *again*," "oh what's he like" said Emily, "I know, I'm just off back home to wait for his call, you still ok for tomorrow? you are still coming, aren't you?" said Sam, "yeah of course," "ok your dad and I will be there about mid-day, ok," "yep that's fine see you then, bye, bye, bye," Emily hangs up.

Samantha arrives home, "sorry Mr Darcy, but he missed the bloody train '*again*'," Mr Darcy just about raises an eye in acknowledgement, shuffles and settles back into another well-earned sleep, he was very much their, 'saggy old cloth cat puss' and they all loved him dearly for it.

Samantha tried Oliver's phone again this time it connected but went to answer machine, "hi this is Oliver, sorry can't take your call just now, but will get back to you as soon as, bye." beeeeeeeeeep, "hello this is your wife, have you forgotten you're supposed to be having a dirty weekend with me? if so, then I'll just have to ask the gardener to come over.........'again'," and Sam hangs up.

Minutes later and the phone go's but not her mobile her land line, "hello Samantha here," "hi Sam its Joe," "hi Joe how's things," "ok not bad," "how's that nutty foal of yours, showing any signs of calming down yet or is he still running you ragged" said Sam, "no he's good, I mean still nutty but hey all's good, is Oliver coming home this weekend?" asked Joe, "oh sore subject, he's only gone and missed the bloody train *'again'* Joe and of all weekends, what with Emily's birthday next week, I told him how important it was," joe laughs, "so you've spoken to Oliver then," "no" said Sam, there was a pause, "Joe, what's up," asked Sam, "Sam turn on the telly," "why what is going on?" "look I'm sure it's all ok but turn the telly on and call me back ok," "ok" said Sam, puzzled.

Joe had known Oliver and Sam for a long time and there was no way he'd miss that train on such an important weekend and if he had he would have been on the phone by now begging for forgiveness, what's happened is Oliver has obviously volunteered to stay and help deal with all the casualties, but he should have at least sent a text to say, Joe had said to herself. Sam flicked on the TV and without having to choose a channel it was there, a grim-faced reporter was saying, "casualties suspected into the tens of dozens, hospital staff are urged to report for duty, central London at a standstill, 'terrorist attack'," Sam's head was spinning, she jumped out of her skin as the phone rang again and she dashed across the living room, snatched up the phone and shouted "Oliver," "no its Joe," "oh Joe," Joe could hear Sam's voice cracking, "I'm coming right now," said Joe.

For the next few hours both Sam and Joe called every number that they could find, they spoke to everyone, but it was impossible to speak to hospitals as the situation was so confusing, no one knew anything, Sam did get through to one of Oliver's colleagues who could confirm that Oliver done his late shift on Thursday into Friday morning because he spoke to him, but as far as he knew Oliver went home shortly after and he didn't mean his digs, but home, home. One scenario that they hadn't thought of and Oliver's colleagues suggested is that Oliver may have been conscripted into the staff of another Hospital in which to help, "is that likely" said Sam, "anything is likely right now Sam, the situation is off the scale". By early evening they had exhausted every line, "look, he's caught up in this, saving lives Sam, you know what he's like," "but why hasn't he called?" "yes, I know but as his colleague said, this is off the scale Sam, he'll be in touch as soon as he can," "look Joe you'd better go, the boys will need feeding," "no not on your nelly Sam, Trevor can look after the boys, I'm staying with you, now I think we need a stiff drink, white or red, Sam sighed deeply, hands on head, "red please, and thanks Joe," "for what," "being here," "you'd do the same," Joe paused….., "are you going to call Emily?" "and say what? I don't know Joe? what do I do?" "ok leave it for now, if she calls, you'll have to play it down, play it by ear, but knowing her she's probably out with friends and has no idea of the situation," "let's hope so" said Sam. "Well, we've done everything we can, we'll just have to sit tight and wait for Oliver," they sat for the rest of the night watching the constant news feed of the unfolding events.

Sam was awoken by the sound of car tires on the stone drive, the tv was still on and still relaying a continuous loop of the events in London the day before. Joe was still asleep at the other end of the sofa as Sam made her way to the kitchen window to take a look at who had driven in and she flicked on the kettle as she passed. Sam prised apart the blind with two fingers and peered out at quite a bright early winters morning and squinted, *oh yeah, I had a glass of wine* she reminds herself.

There heading for the door was a man and a woman in their late twenty's early thirties, dressed in suits, the lady in fact was in a trouser suit and Sam had to think whether she had made and forgotten an appointment with BEF (British Equestrian Federation), she was sure she hadn't and she most certainly didn't need double glazing, and nor for her soul to be saved. The doorbell rang and Sam moved into the hall just as Joe opened an adjacent door, "who's that?" asked Joe,

"I have no idea, the kettles on," said Sam. As Sam opens the door, she was greeted with a "good morning," from the two visitors and before she could reply the man asked "Samantha Williams?" "yes, that's me," and in unison as if rehearsed both the man and woman reached into their jacket pockets and produced badges, "I'm DS Daniel Hardiman and this is my colleague DC Rebecca Simons, Bury St Edmunds Central Police station, may we come in please." Sam staggered backwards her hands to her face and muttered. "it's Oliver, isn't it!?" at this point Sam is joined by Joe who immediately took in the scene and said to Sam "wait Sam. It could be anything," "and you are Madam?" asked DS Hardiman, "I'm Joe, a family friend," "good" replied Hardiman, which seemed only to confirm Sam's worst suspicions, "may we come in?" "oh yes, sorry" said Sam, "please do," the officers were led to the snug in which Sam and Joe had spent the night, the tv was switched off, "would you like some tea?" said Sam and the two officers briefly looked at one another, "no that's fine, but thank you," it was the first time the women officer had spoken.

"It's about Oliver, isn't it, is he hurt!?" asked Sam, the strain in her voice quite audible, "can I confirm that Oliver Williams is your husband?" ask DC Simons, "YES! Oliver is my husband, now what's wrong with him, please?" snapped Sam, not meaning to be sharp, "I am very sorry to have to inform you Samantha, but Oliver was killed yesterday morning in London."

From the word 'sorry' Sam physically collapsed into the sofa, hands to face, and a large guttural scream came out from within her that shocked all present, Joe on recovering slid in alongside Sam and threw both arms around her, Joe began to ask questions that Sam was in no condition To do, "your referring to the terrorist attack in Covent Garden, aren't you?" "we cannot at this time confirm it was a terrorist attack" said DS Hardiman, "but you can confirm that Oliver was caught up in it, how? "asked Joe, "Oliver was identified at the scene by his personal belongings and by two eyewitnesses," "what eyewitness?" ask Joe, "at the time of the second explosion," Hardiman began, "so, it was a terrorist attack," said Joe and Hardiman gave Joe a look that said, please, don't make this any more difficult than it is, Joe quietened, "at the time of the second explosion, Oliver had identified himself to the Assistant commissioner of the Met, his party had arrived to assess the situation, those who survived from that party identified Oliver," "and the second," asked Joe, "was an off-duty nurse from St Bart's who had assisted Oliver with caring for the victims of the first explosion" said Hardiman, out from under a curled-up Sam came a shaky voice that asked, "and, how is she?" "I'm sorry" asked Hardiman, "the nurse, is she ok," asked Sam, "yes" said Hardiman, "apart from shock and some scratches, she's ok," 'good," said Sam, "I'd like to thank her," everyone a bit taken back at Sam's concern for others at a time like this. Sam dried her eyes, sniffed and as though nothing had just happened, she asked, "would everyone like that tea now?" Joe immediately jumps up and says, "no I'll do that" and disappeared into the kitchen.

"Samantha" said DC Simons, "I'm Rebecca and I'm with the family support unit and will be with you over the next few weeks, well, for as long as you need us" she said, "but why? "said Sam. "well I'm here to give help and support at this difficult time, but also to give advice and Protection," "protection? From what, terrorists?" Sam said with some surprise, "no, Samantha, it has more to do with media attention, I'm afraid," Hardiman leaned in and said, "we'll also need you to identify Oliver's body as soon as is possible," "Why? you just said that it was Oliver" said Sam, "yes, I'm afraid its procedure, a family member has to formally identify the body," "so, it's possible that it may not be Oliver," said Sam, the officers stared blankly and thankfully just then Joe came back into the room with a tray of tea.

Sam shot to her feet, almost spilling her mug of tea that was in hand and proclaimed, almost at a shout, "Emily." A short while later Joe came off the phone having just spoken to the head of Thrashams, Dr Davis. Joe had to relay the sad news and Dr Davis immediately took charge at his end, he would personally make sure that Emily would be kept busy with the Saturday morning study club that was run in the library, this wasn't that difficult to organise as Emily could often be found there on a Saturday helping other students with their studies. After a little 'two and throw' between Sam, Joe and Rebecca, it was eventually agreed that they would take Sam's car and Joe would drive, Rebecca would accompany them to the school, but they were not to come into the school when Sam broke the news to Emily, they agreed. DS Hardiman jumped into his car and returned to Bury central to make his reports, Rebecca Joe and Sam readied themselves for the journey to Norfolk.

Sam was glad that Rebecca chose to sit in the back with her as it would have seemed a little lonely there by herself. Sam sat in silence as the Suffolk then Norfolk countryside rolled by. The radio had been turned off rather sharply the moment a news report came on, but Sam was glad of the peace, it gave her time to process all that had just happened, and although there was this thought, a glimmer that perhaps it wasn't Oliver, *what if they had gotten it wrong? and he was lying in a hospital bed somewhere unable to communicate,* but she knew, she knew that it was him, because running into harm's way to help others was just the thing Oliver would have done.

They reached the long chip stone drive of Thrashams around eleven and driving up to the rather grand facade of the school led Sam back to happier times over the last two years, Emily's academic as well as sporting achievements and she knew Emily had truly loved it here and now she was about to taint all of that. As they pulled up Dr Davis came through the door and down the steps to greet them all, but this time, forlornly. "Samantha, I'm so sorry to hear the news" the Doctor said whilst gripping her hand with both of his in an attempt at comforting her, Sam just nodded. "I've asked for Emily come to my study and wait for me there, I'll take you directly," Joe and Rebecca did as they were asked and stayed with the car. Sam followed the Doctor down a number of twisting and turning corridors that eventually led to his office that was situated on the ground floor at the back of this grand country house. The Doctor paused at a large oak door and before turning the handle to open gave Sam an indication that told her that Emily was just beyond, and Sam had to take a deep breath to steady herself.

Emily had been led into the room some ten minutes before and rather than just sitting she let her curiosity get the better of her and she was now scanning the Doctors private collection of books with some amusement, there was of course the expected academic books but also a good sprinkle of reads just for enjoyment, which she liked to see.

The door clicked and Emily spun around to see her Mother walk in as the Doctor held the door, "Mum, what are you doing here so early?" without saying anything Sam walked to her Daughter and hugged her, "Mum?" said Emily again, Sam gestured to the French doors that lead to an ornate garden and the Doctor said "of course, please," and he opened them for her and Emily to go through. The Doctor gently closed the doors behind them and watched as they walked hand in hand a few yards onto the manicured lawn and beneath a canopy of cedar trees, Sam turned to Emily and holding her hands began to speak, the Doctor could not hear what Sam was saying and neither did he want to that would have been just too much, but from the closed door he saw the expression on Emily's face change and as she slipped to her knee's, arms flung around the backs of her Mum's legs, her body jerked and convulsed as she struggled to heave breath into her body and push grief and shock out, she buried her head into her mother's stomach and sobbed, the doctor had to rip himself from the doors and now stood steading himself at his desk barely able to hold back his own tears.

On the journey home Rebecca sat up front, Sam in the back with Emily laid across the seats with her head in Sam's lap and not very much was said. On reaching home, Sam got Emily in and settled, and Rebecca informed her that if She wished and wanted, Rebecca would return the following morning and take her to London to identify Oliver, Sam agreed that this should be done as quickly as possible, Sam needed to see Oliver as soon as she could, a time was agreed and Rebecca left. Sam turned to Joe and thanked her, the two women hugged and Joe said, "I'd better go and check on my lot, see if their still?" and stopped herself from saying 'alive', "I'm so sorry, I didn't mean to say that," "It's ok Joe, I still can't quite believe it too," "I'll check in with you later, "and Joe left, and, on her return home, she hugged all her family much to the complaints of her boys who just wanted to know what there was to eat and she felt blessed.

Emily had insisted on coming to London with Sam and Rebecca despite the reason for the trip and quietly Sam was glad she was coming, she didn't like the idea of her being left alone in the cottage with too much time to think. However, on arrival at the morgue Emily decided that she didn't want to see her father and felt bad that she wouldn't be there to support her mother, something Sam was also glad of, she would rather Emily stayed in the waiting room and remember her father from the good times before. Sam was led into small room with a large single glass panel on one side, Rebecca had explained that when Sam was ready the curtain would be pulled back and she would see Oliver on a hospital gurney, she could take her time or if it were too much just say and they will draw the curtains again. Sam nodded and indicated to Rebecca that she was ready, well, as ready as she could be. Rebecca pressed a buzzer to one side of the window that Sam hadn't noticed and immediately the curtain began to slide sideways.

There on a gurney was the form of a human under a white sheet, a masked member of staff having received a nod from Rebecca moved to one side of the gurney and gently folded down the sheet to chest level, Sam gasped, and there was Oliver, Sam recognised him instantly and in that instance all hope was dashed of any thought that it may not have been him, this thought now replaced with the feeling that although he was right there, he was in fact not dead as he looked so peaceful, at rest, as though he were asleep, she hadn't expected for him to look so good, she hadn't known what to expect of someone who had been in an explosion, but he had not a mark on him. It finally hit Sam that the man she had spent most of her entire life with was now still, lifeless and cold before her. For the two of them had been so close, physically, mentally and emotionally, and to have had so little time of late to say just how much she truly loved him, to be stood here now not able to speak, to touch, to hold a hand and to just say in a whisper, sleep now my darling, for you are safe, crushed her, damn this glass barrier, her head dropped as she placed both hands on the glass and as tears cascaded to the floor, she felt her legs go, Rebecca lurched forward and just caught Sam before she collapsed, placing one arm under her rib cage and another at her back and sat Sam in a chair just behind, Rebecca nodded at the staff and the curtain slid back, and so, the image of Oliver slid away, to forever be at the forefront of Samantha's mind. Sam composed herself and re-joined Emily in the waiting room whilst they waited for Rebecca and she recounted to Emily just how unhurt and at peace her father had looked.

Rebecca appeared carrying a large opaque plastic evidence bag, "what's that?" asked Sam "these are Oliver's personal effects for you to take home now," Sam again nodded. The trip back home to Suffolk was once again a solemn one and not very much was said.

The day of the Funeral

It had been two weeks since her mother and Emily had gone to the morgue in London to identify her father. The first few days and nights had been spent in pyjamas, not really eating anything, walking from one room to the next, recounting and replaying back images of her father at differing times, such as charades at Christmas, and picking up objects such as books and thinking to herself, *he was the last person to touch this,* and holding that object to her cheek or chest.

A number of people from the village dropped by to offer their condolences and of course Joe came by, which was in fact appreciated as she was a small glimpse of normality and a breath of fresh air into an environment that felt as though it was becoming stagnant, and it didn't hurt that she also brought with her milk and bread and a supply of wine for mum, she guessed that was how her mother was going to cope with this, it was however deemed that Emily should be assisted in coping in an entirely different way, one of the callers was their family Doctor, Dr Hendricks. After some discussions with her mother, it was determined that it would be good for Emily to take some mild sedatives to help her cope with the situation and, she didn't argue, she couldn't, there was not a fight within her at this time and besides perhaps the drugs may help her sleep.

As much as time seemed to drag over those two weeks and before they felt they had time to be ready, the day of the funeral was upon them, *they were never going to be ready*, what an absurd thought, *who would be ready for her own father's funeral?* Emily said to herself whilst putting on clothes of an all dark nature in design and colour. The cars were to pick them up at Willow Cottage at around 10:45am for the 11am start of service and as if on que the previous night the first of that winters snow came down leaving a white blanket of some six inches. Oliver had, unbeknown to Samantha, requested a funeral at the local church in Owlsden. Samantha was not entirely surprised at having no knowledge of these arrangements, she guessed that Oliver hadn't wanted to broach such a situation with her, deeming it unnecessary as they were still both quite youthful and any thought of their demise was confined to them both being of old age and thus, plenty of time for such conversations later, and not as a result of some deluded, mindless terrorist attack. Samantha damned those monsters to the darkest depths of hell. "The cars are here," said Emily as she pops her head around the doorway of her mother's room, "ok, I'm just about ready, let's take a look at you," said Sam, Emily reluctantly pulled herself from around the door and into the room, "you look lovely" said Sam, "Mum this isn't a fashion parade, and I'm sure Dads not going to worry too much how we look," "oh I'm sure he would darling," said Sam, "you look lovely too Mum" said Emily and the two of them hugged, and as the two parted Emily said, "stay close to me today please," and Sam smiled and said "of course" as she held Emily's face.

It seemed silly to travel such a short distance by car to the church and Emily would have normally requested they walked but in light of the weather it was of course prudent to travel by car. Sam and Emily climbed into the back of a black funeral car parked behind the hearse, the driver was startled as the back door opened, he was still sat in the driver's seat and felt a little embarrassed as he was supposed to open the door for them, he leaned over and switched off the radio, "could you leave that on please" asked Emily, and the driver was all too pleased to, Emily wanted to experience everything of this day, good and bad. As they pulled away following the hearse, the reporter on the radio was talking of how the President of the United States had signed a bill to extend the US Marines Corp by a further division, that of 'Space Marines' and Emily couldn't help but think, *what are they expecting to find in space that needs armed Marines.?*

The next report was of course concerning the attack two weeks previous, there hadn't been much else on the news of late. The reporter was saying that those who had been in a critical condition were now deemed to be off that list and on their way to recovery. That now left fifty-two dead, of which there was eight Paramedics and three Police officers, one of which was Jack Spinner Assistant Commissioner, Metropolitan Police and two hundred and five injured. Of the two attackers, it would seem they were known to the authorities and had been traced to properties in the midlands, these having been raided by anti-terrorist officers and had subsequently been searched. Most concerning to the authorities was the planning and time of the attacks.

The two bombs were detonated separately and from elevated platforms part way up the stairs at either ends and in front of the food hall. The first was to kill and injure as many civilians as possible, the second was deliberately detonated sometime later with the intension of catching as many first responders as possible. The bombs themselves were of concern too, for their design and construction had not been seen since the days of the IRA. Around the explosive core was a combination of three-inch nails and two-inch bolts that had all been painstakingly placed top to tail to give maximum effect as they span through the air. But there was one other ingredient that they had used, not seen before, that of marbles, kids toy glass marbles that had also been tightly packed around the explosive core. The effect of these glass marbles on impact with human flesh and bone were to shatter with devastatingly horrific effect, the recipient needing hours of surgery to try and remove all the shards some of which had become molten during the explosion. It was assumed that the use of marble was a test to see if they could avoid metal detection and thus there was concern for future attacks and targets. The location had also been carefully thought through not just because Covent Garden had a glass ceiling which did what was expected of it at the time of the explosion but also because Covent Garden is in line of sight of both the Houses of Parliament and Buckingham Palace and the plume of smoke that the explosion created would have been clearly seen by both. Although the attack had not come on a day of religious celebration, it was clear that it was an attack upon our way of life, upon what connects us all, caring, understanding, and love. *This day will forever be known in history, in infamy as The St Valentine's Day Massacre of London.*

They had turned the corner into the main street of the village passed The Fox and hounds Inn and there in front upon a hill was St Peters Church, constructed by the Normans almost one thousand years before and looking resplendent in its cloak of white snow. But what took Sam and Emily by surprise was the scene before them, it would seem that all three hundred of the inhabitants of Owlsden Village had come out to line the street and as they passed old men doffed their caps and Mums crossed themselves and children clapped solemnly, Sam had promised herself not to cry too much but on seeing this out pouring of respect for Oliver made her instantly well up.

Oliver was of Irish descendants and although a Catholic he wasn't practising and would wander into a church more for the architecture than to pray. There would be no family coming from home as parents on both sides were now dead and whatever family Oliver now had he'd lost touch with many years ago. The Rt. Rev Peter Day had been invited from the Bury St Edmunds King and Martyr Catholic Parish to take the service. As Sam and Emily took their positions by the freshly dug grave the small graveyard filled to capacity. Reverend Day gave a lovely sermon and Sam couldn't believe he had come to know so much about Oliver, he talked of *a man, of compassion, who would put all before his own needs and safety,* something all too apparent the day of the attack.

The two police officers Daniel and Rebecca were present, and Sam found out later that they had already informed the reporters and the BBC news crew from Norwich that there were to be no interviews and to keep their distance, and to their credit they did. Sam and Emily stood arm in arm, and at that moment they were invited to come forward and place a flower each onto the top of the coffin, the snow began to fall gently covering the coffin lid as it was lowered into the ground.

Emily could not watch and at this point looking away across the graveyard and through the falling flakes, she made out the image of a large white owl watching the proceedings, sat high above in an old oak tree close to the entrance of the church.

As the crowds dispersed Sam and Emily stayed behind to thank the reverend and those of note such as some of Oliver's work colleagues. Sam noticed a young woman she did not recognise who had stood to one side politely waiting for her chance to come forward. She eventually did and with outstretched hand said, "hello Mrs Williams, I'm Heather, the nurse that assisted Oliver on that day," Sam and Heather embraced as though they were long lost friends and as they parted Sam holding the young woman's hands said "thank you, thank you so much," "no Mrs Williams," "please call me Sam," "no Sam, I only had the privilege of knowing Oliver for such a short time, but it was obvious what a wonderful man he was, and I knew I had to be here today just to let you know that," "will you come to the wake? it's at the Fox just down there on the left, I would like to speak to you more, over a drink, perhaps?" "yes of course, I'd love to, I'll see you there" said Heather. Sam and Emily walked the short distance to the Fox to try and regain their composure, which was once more dashed as on entering a packed pub of locals, farmers, farm hands and bikers, all stood and applauded.

The landlord an Irishman himself called Pat informed Sam that there was to be no charge for the buffet, it was the least he could do for a fellow country man and local hero, Sam wasn't too sure that Oliver would have gone along with the hero thing, but it was appreciated never the less. Sam introduced Emily to Heather, and they found a corner and chatted for an hour. Heather left shortly after as she had to get back to London and after a polite while Sam and Emily stood, thanked everyone and bid them a good evening, all stood and raised a glass.

Sam and Emily crunched the short distance in moon lit darkness back down the hill towards Willow Cottage, holding on to one another for both physical and emotional support. To inhale meant there came the sting in their lungs of cold weather and the moon illuminated the snow-covered fields and there was a hush upon the land a stillness that only a white blanket such as this could bring, and they let go of that day's pent up emotion and cried with every step.

Emily looked at a heaven of stars above them and she got the over whelming feeling that someone was watching them, was her father here?

Cometh the Count

Baghdad 1623

Pierre Bourbonne Count De Livron, Champagne, southern France found himself languishing in the camp of Shah Abbas, I ruler of the Safavid Persian Empire, beneath the Baghdad city walls.

The count had some months previous offered his sword for a sum, to Shah Abbas I to assist with the fight against those of the Ottoman Empire who had made Baghdad a city of many thousands, their centre for controlling the lands there abouts. The count was a long way from home, a home that despite its proximity to the boarder of Spain was at this time of year that of a more comfortable and clement climate. Here, in the desert was as far from comfortable as could be, this only adding to the counts frustration, for in these weeks had seen him called to action on too few occasions for his liking and because of this, the count felt that he had not the opportunity to exercise his sword arm on nearly enough opportunities.

The few skirmishes in which he was able to show off his prowess and skilfulness as a sword man was enough for those who were there to witness, to proclaim the sheer barbarity and ferociousness of this man in combat, it was said, that, *it was not thy enemy that was to be feared whence charging into battle alongside the count, for his sword holds no prejudice, whether thy be friend or foe.'* The Persian's in their native tongue had come to call the count 'Daeva,' a god that had been cast out, a god that promotes chaos and destruction, 'The Devil,' demon, a monster. On such occasions when they had engaged the enemy, the count would be the last to leave the battlefield, the last to return to camp, he, his sword and armament, that, usually of a black in colour would now be discoloured and drenched in the blood of the slain.

On those days when fighting was not required, he would assist in training the men of Shah Abbas I and readying himself and his weapons. 'ARMOURER' came the cry from the count as he left his tent, 'ARMOURER," where the damn are you?' the armourer came scurrying over, "my Lord I am here," the armourer had within his hands a sheathed sword and now held this out, "ahhh you have my sword, I see," "yes my lord," "did you follow my instruction armourer," "yes, my lord, with the keenest of eye," "keen you say, and what of the blade, is it keen also." The collective Knights and Nobles around the fire looked on with some amusement. "Yes, my Lord the blade is as keen as my willingness to live" the armourer hangs his head, now instantly and deeply regretted his, possibly, last comment, as the collective chuckles.

The count required of his sword that the last six inches; the tip of the sword was razor sharp for slashing an opponent or as the count had become famous for, cleaving a man clean in half.

As for the rest of the sword, although most certainly not blunt, it did not need to have such a keen edge as this part of the sword would be used to break a man's arms or legs, on occasion the count had been known to do just that, to circle a man carefully placing strikes that would eventually leave a man rendered helpless upon the sand unable to raise themselves and the count would, depending on his mood at the time would either finish them off or leave them for the vultures.

"Keenness to live, you say armourer, shall we put that to the test?" a smile on the count's lips, the collective ceased to be amused as if they now sense the deadliness of the situation, some stood as if to step in at the last moment to save the armourer, after all, the fellow was of use.

The armourer now visibly shaking, gulped, mouth dry unable to speak. The count spun on his heals and walked a short distance toward a camel that was laden with stores and tethered to a palm tree, with one seemingly casual swing the count severed the head of the camel from its body, its legs holding briefly before the animal slumped into the ground, the warm sand eagerly soaking up the blood now spirting from its neck. The collective Knights and Nobles now roaring with laughter, perhaps more to do with relief than amusement. The two tradesmen whose camel it had been now complaining bitterly, but in a subservient manner towards the count who without looking tossed the tradesman a coin, for the counts glare was now fixed once again upon the armourer, "here armourer, for a job well done," and the count tosses another coin in his direction, to a chorus from the collective behind him of, "come Count, let us drink."

January 1624

The count receives the news he had been waiting for, Shah Abbas I gives orders that the city walls were to be breached and Baghdad taken. Before the sun rise on that following day Abbas's army swarmed into the city, the count at its head, there were to follow two days of fighting in which most men would in an orderly fashion retreat temporarily from the field of battle to regroup and take on food and water, but not the count, from the first days break to the downing of the sun on that last day the count did not cease in his pursuit of pray, from plaza to plaza, street to street, house to house the count slashed, stabbed and beat anything and everything that stood within his path.

On surveying the cruel and sad scene of this once great city, Shah Abbas I called upon the Ottoman Empire to form a temporary truce between them. The count found that the very men about him would no longer look him in the eye, preferring to avert their gaze upon the floor whenever he approached. Shah Abbas I found the count bathing his sore and swollen hands in a water trough, "Ahh count, your work here is done Sir, I trust you shall have a safe and speedy journey from my country," as he handed the count a purse of gold, and thus, this adventure ceases to be no more, *off to hunting grounds new*, thought the count.

The count was born in 1603 in Livron in Southern France to gentry parents who owned a good deal of land in that area and who also had a tentative and distant claim to the Royal throne of France. Although small in stature he was strong and had the speed and agility of a black mamba snake, his hair was that of tassels and black as a raven. His features were just as dark, and he sported a moustache that was waxed at the end and a small tuft of hair in a triangular formation just below his bottom lip. The count would predominantly wear black clothing, not that this had anything to do with the fashion of the day, the Musketeer look was very in, but it had more to do with the fact that blood did not show up upon black so readily. He, in the right company could be charming as any French man can be but would prefer to shun such social interaction wherever possible, finding that *people can be so cumbersome and awkward, and really rather tiresome.* So, it came as no surprise that the count preferred to travel alone, by horseback, leading another horse laden with stores. The count was not fearful of bandits such was his confidence in his own fighting ability and awareness, that at times he would relish the idea of an ambush. The count, although his primary weapon and that of preference was his beloved sword would also carry two French made wheel-lock pistols and a blunderbuss for just such an occasion should it have happened, but he frowned on such a method of dispatching an enemy, shooting a man at distance*, for where is the sport in that?* He would also carry a number of daggers placed about his person, but it was his stance, his demeanour that would ward people off the moment they eyed him.

As the count made his way up through Spain, he would on occasion pay for that night's lodgings and food by offering a duel to the local strong arms, and thugs, not to the death, of course, he would have probably found his way barred at some point if he had left a trail of bodies behind him, but it was also good practice. However, on one occasion he had thrown down the gauntlet to one of these local ruffians and had announced to the gathering crowd that he was "Pierre Bourbonne Count De Livron fifty second in line to the throne of France," and on turning his back to his opponent and readying himself to duel he hears the man say, "you have lofty delusions of grandeur Sir, shame your stature was not of the Same," a chuckle comes from the crowd, the count raised his sword in salute, momentarily closes his eyes and mutters to himself, "yes, this one shall die."

The count arrived back in his homeland of southern France in 1626, to religious and political chaos. The French king Louis XIII, a Catholic, was at odds with the Huguenot rebellion led by The Duke Henri De Rohan, Protestant. The Huguenots formed a strong hold in the city of

La Rochelle, a city of some thirty thousand inhabitants, on the south west coast of France which had become besieged by the king's Royal forces. In the same year Walter Montagu was despatched to France by the then King of England, Charles I to contact dissident French nobleman and to rally them in support of Henri De Rohan at La Rochelle. It was around this time that the count sort council with Montagu and after some negotiations that were said to have reached the ear of the King of England, the count found himself in the employ of the English.

The king of England had become concerned with the build-up of French military might of recent, in particular its Navy and the close ties it was forming with Spain. The count, when asked of his religion, reportedly commented, *I worship the God that pays best*, and when asked of his thoughts on fighting his fellow countrymen, he laughed and said, *they'll bleed just like any other.*

In June of 1627 The King, Charles I sent a fleet of some eighty ships to the region of La Rochelle under the command of his favourite, George Villiers, 1st Duke of Buckingham. The count joined this force in September and was heavily involved with the landings on the Isle of Ile De Re and the subsequent attacks upon St Martin, it was commented in despatches of the time that, *The Count de Livron most certainly lived up to his reputation.* It wasn't long after the French Kings forces were victorious and routed the Huguenots from La Rochelle and our count finds himself departing for England, for as to have stayed in France would have most certainly, resulted in the parting of his head from his neck. As pre-agreed with The King of England the count was to be given lands and made Lord of that manor, that some amongst the Royal court had expressed concern as to the sensibility of such an act of the King who in response said that, "in light of recent events both home and abroad it may Prove prudent to have such men as the count close to one's side?" And so, it was that in early 1628 the count de Livron arrived in the county of Suffolk and the very sleepy hamlet of Owlsden.

The count received one hundred hectares of arable Suffolk land, which on reflection was not that much but did make him the largest landowner in the area and thus Lord, if all but in name.

The count wasted no time in surveying the land and came across a quite unusual land anomaly in the form of a large diamond water formation that the count immediately saw as making a particularly good defensive position in which to site his grand manor house.

In that same year, The Count took a wife, Kathrine, a good-looking woman, from good French stock, but The Count was not in love, it was more a union of convenience, however he did admire Kathrine's ambitiousness in wishing to return to French high society and shortly after Kathrine bore him a son who he named Louis after his father. Louis would in time marry into the Royal Courts of Europe and hence hale the Counts return. The manor was constructed having brought large oak timbers from France and the tradesman also from his homeland to build this grand structure. But first a bridge had to be erected in which to reach the Island and the count thought it curious as to the practicality and use of such a piece of land, what with it being locked by water. Over the coming years the count settled into a life less interesting as it was before and thus had to busy himself with building his empire, all be it small and there followed upon his land an abattoir, a brewery and the courthouse all constructed along the lane that led to the manor. There were also stables and an assortment of out buildings to compliment the farming of his land, land in which he did employ a good many men to toil upon and a handful of staff at the manor. By 1645 The counts empire was now complete, the manor house long so as had the grounds that were now mature. Apart from the beams and some finishing materials and furniture a good deal did in fact come from local sources such as the brick that was made with the local clay, which was unusual in that it contained minerals that were usually found at greater depth which made for a particularly strong brick and very red in colour.

The manor house was finished in such a way that although was not a typical looking French chateau, it would, however, strike the casual observer that this was not a locally designed and built property. On leaving the manor you would cross the bridge which spanned the moat some fifteen feet, the count had seen to it that if necessity called for, two thirds of the bridge from the manor side could be raised in a similar fashion as a draw bridge, a request that had the counts work man perplexed as to the reason when ordered to construct, asking one another as to what this count was expecting to come from over the hill to warrant such a thing. On leaving the bridge, one stepped onto the drive that led to the lane, to your front and right side were ornate gardens with a number of foreign species of plant and tree, beyond this were the stables, farm buildings and then a large paddock. To the left on leaving the bridge were the gardens that supplied the manors kitchen and again the gardeners were very proud not only of the amounts that they could produce but also the variety of fruits and vegetables. Leaving the main gates to the manor you would turn left onto the lane and not far along you would come to the brewery, timber framed and red brick construction, it had a number of Large rooms for both production and storage of the beer that was brewed there, it was reached by a small bridge construction that spanned the stream that ran alongside the lane. Further up and again on the left you would find the courthouse, accessed again over the stream, surrounded by willow trees, this was again timber and brick, and consisted of just a ground floor, however the outside walls were high with a pitched roof of tiles which gave the impression that the building had an upstairs. There was a door and window lane side and a further door on the left-hand side of the property that led into a garden. Yards from the left-hand door was a pond that had a large and quite unusual oak tree by its side, its trunk was gnarled and twisted. Further down the garden towards the brewery was a second pond that was never used. The interior of the courthouse was plain plastered walls, the roof timbers were exposed, a large opening in the roof directly above a central firepit in the floor. There were simple wooden benches in rows as one walked in, the isle leading to a raised platform on which sat a long table and chairs, to its left was the dock the accused would stand in. High up upon the walls a gallery had been constructed on three sides and about three feet wide so people could look down on the proceedings, a staircase in the corner would lead you up. Leaving the courthouse and left up the hill you would come to the abattoir, again on the left over the stream, and like the brewery was constructed for commerce use and thus had very little in the way of comfort, perhaps a building of such purpose should and would never have anything to do with such words as comfort considering it was the last thing a great many animals did see. On the day of slaughter, usually a Friday, the animals would be herded and corralled on site and one by one they would meet their end, gutted and portioned, the majority of the meat sent that day to the manor to be hung, cured or cooked to preserve.

Some meat mostly scrag end would be sold to locals, there then began the most undesirable part of the job that of cleaning down the scenes of slaughter with brooms and many a bucket of water. The remains would be swept and swilled across the yard and into the stream in a hope that shortly a down pour of rain would come to wash this vile heap away before it brought about a stench that only decaying and rotting blood, guts and entrails can bring. Further on up the lane and you come to a junction and turning left you came to the forge and the Fox and hounds Inn to one side, this heralds the centre of the village and a small collection of homes and just beyond is the Church of St Peter. The village had a small number of inhabitants, most if not, all worked for the Count.

The village was sleepy to say the least, it could be said that time had passed Owlsden by, but it would seem that its remote and isolated location meant that nothing had happened here and for many a year not since the invasion of the Roman empire in 43 AD which was initially seen off by the Iceni tribe and their Queen Boudicca, that tall strong wild haired woman. Their initial success in defending this quiet corner of Suffolk inevitably led to their ultimate defeat at the hands of a far superior military might of the Roman legions. There then followed thousands of years of peace and tranquillity the like of which the count was now finding very hard to comprehend and come to terms with. He was restless, he had fought all across Europe and into north Africa and swash buckled his way back again, and now he had become tired, tired of this mundane, tired of the slowness and pace of life here, he had become weak, lazy, slovenly, his sword arm had become restless and yearned for action.

In charge of the everyday running of the counts empire, mundane or not was Medea, she had been the housekeeper at the manor from the very start, it could not be remembered how she first came to be in the employment of the count, but it would seem that she had always been there. Medea although strict when it came to the affairs of the estate and the running of the manor was a kindly woman, someone that one could turn to for advice and in moments of crisis, for she seemed to have a worldly knowledge, particularly when it came to matters of the body and its wellbeing, quick to hand one a potion of sorts to cure all ailments. Medea was tall for a woman of those times and beautiful in a plain sort of way, with long, straight shiny hair that was as black as midnight, and eyes that at times seemed all the darker, but a smile that would brighten any room, she had indeed a presence about her. Medea enjoyed the company of all her staff at the manor and that of the farm and stables, but it was one who did indeed hold a special place in her affections, that of little Annie Wright.

Annie was at that time about to turn sixteen, she was short, barely five feet in stocking feet with long, brilliant blonde curly hair that hung about her shoulders. Annie was not the shy retiring type, she was feisty, her mother and father who both worked on the estate would freely admit that Annie was a hand full and had always been so.

She certainly had a mind of her own and at times would often be heard to say exactly what she thought, which would, of course get her into much trouble. Despite her tender years Annie had developed into a voluptuous young woman, but it was her love of life that Medea adored, Annie had bags of energy and enthusiasm, running bare foot from one place to another, bursting into rooms and taking people by surprise, she had spirit, a spark that could not be put out and Medea loved being in her company, even when sometimes it was with some frustration that she looked at Annie through the eyes of a doting mother. Annie was coming of age and had caught the eye of many a young man in the village and there abouts. But it was for only one set of eyes that she had any interest of and that was of Louis the counts eighteen-year-old son. Their admiring gaze had glanced upon one another on many an occasion when Annie was flittering about the manor and stable yards.

It was on one sunny afternoon that Louis on horseback had come across Annie in the lane returning from an errand for Medea. "Good day to you my lady" said Louis, "and a good day to you to good sir" said Annie, Louis was of a good height and athletic build with neat blonde hair and was clean shaved, he had taken after his mother more so then that of the count and it would seem not just in looks for he had a placid demeanour about him, although he could handle a sword, he had of course been tutored by his father from an early age, the lad had become fascinated in the day to day season by season routines of the land and farming, spending inordinate amount of time in the company of the farm manager Thomas as opposed to his fathers. "Pray what brings you here unaccompanied my lady?" "an errand sir for mistress Medea" "I do beg of you your pardon my lady for where are my manners, I am Louis Bourbonne son to the Count De Livron and lord of this manor," Annie giggled at this introduction, for she knew all too well who he was, "I do know who you are sir, and I am Annie Wright, and am very pleased to make your acquaintance," she curtsy's and there then followed an awkward silence brought about by Louis realising that his introduction had been slightly overstated, "do you know that meadow" said Annie, "that I do" said Louis, "they say it holds a particularly good vantage point in which to admire the setting of the sun" said Annie, eyebrows raised, Louis wishing to redeem himself leant down from his saddle and scooped little Annie up and sat her side saddle in front of him, their noses almost touching, both with broad grins upon their faces, Louis wrapped his arms about her and gripping onto the reins they trotted off in the direction of the meadow.

The sunset from the meadow was indeed idyllic and the two young lovers relaxed in each other's company as they spoke of growing up and families, perhaps more so Annie then Louis.

All of a sudden Annie proclaimed, wide eyed "I'm late for mistress Medea" and went to slide from the saddle and then paused as she placed a hand on Louis's face leaned forward and kissed his lips, just once but slowly and passionately, pulling away she giggled, slides from the horse and laughing she runs for the meadow entrance in the direction of the manor, louis struggling to get the horse to respond, it wishing to continue to feed on the lush grasses of the meadow. He finally got the horses attention and went to turn and give chase, but it was all too late for Annie was gone and he was left with the most incredible feelings, that of a young man who had just experienced the first twangs of love played upon his heart.

The Coven

From the moment the count had laid the first timbers in the construction of the bridge, the bridge that once created would break the spell and allow for the first time in centuries mere mortals to step upon that land and threaten the very sanctuary of the 'holdfast' and the 'elemental' itself, that force, the very essence of primeval power that laid hidden in the Caverns and tunnels beneath, that which she and the coven had stood and diligently guarded for time in memorial.

Medea called for the coven to come together on that night, a night of no moon and they entered the tunnels via one of the many hidden entrances, the eight dark hooded figures, unspeaking, silent they slid beneath the earth and took their places at the standing stones that formed the circle of North, South, East and West and the four quadrants between. The cavern was large with a low ceiling and was lit by burning torches hung upon the walls. The coven now facing one another, still hooded, still, silent, waiting. Medea stood at the northern stone, the element of sun and without a word she lowered her hood and gestured to the other witches to do the same.

To Medea's left and moving anti clockwise was stood.

Theia the element of wind was from Ancient Egypt and stands at the north eastern standing stone.

Ember the element of fire, a tall strong warrior woman from darkest Africa.

Lupia the element of the beast or animal and was from the Nenets, native's to northern arctic Russia.

Selene, element of the moon and was Mayan.

Onatah, element of earth, a Native American Indian, and daughter of the great Cherokee tribes.

Atalanta the element of water and was from Atlantis.

Bata, the element of wood and was from the Amazon.

All the witches were bound and connected by the ninth and final element, the force that lay beneath their feet, the power, the very spark of life itself.

 The Elemental.

Medea spoke "for centuries now my sisters, we have safeguarded the 'stronghold' and the 'elemental' from being disturbed and discovered by humans, we have even fought to protect one from another."

"We have now a man, a count who has laid claim to the very lands above us, who has built a dwelling to house him and his household, threatening our charge, and the very task that we have been given by the creators." "what shall we do" asked Selene, witch of the moon, and before Medea could answer, Ember, witch of fire, announced "let us kill him and all his house," "no, we shall not" said Medea, "for he has favour with the king of these lands, and we would do best not to draw attention to our 'stronghold' and thus 'the coven', I shall infiltrate this man's household and watch from within and thus will be able to summon you my sisters in a timely fashion should we deem it necessary to snuff out these trespassers, the element of the beast, Lupia shall remain here with me, the rest of you return to the 'four points' and resume thy quest, and I shall keep you all informed from afar, blessed be, my sisters and good speed."

The collective embraced and one by one slid into the darkness as silently as they had come.

Medea

From before the time that man first raised his troubled head and began to walk these lands upright, Medea was there, all seeing, all hearing, feeling those growing pains, ever willing to guide, to take their hand and lead these stumbling creatures in their first faltering steps along the path of enlightenment to reach that higher plain of thought and consciousness.

Medea came to this world 6768 years ago and sort council and courted favour with all the great civilisations of the world as it was then, including those that modern-day men of classical antiquity have to this day no knowledge nor understanding of, such as the great civilisation of Atlantis and the cultures of Lemuria and Rama.

Medea had sort to influence the Mesopotamians, Indus, Egyptian, Maya, Chinese, Greek, Persian, Roman, Aztec and Inca civilisations and had some success to varying degrees, if only to be mentioned in their ancient scripts and hieroglyphics. But it was to no avail, as this creature, this human would always resort to one of its very basic and primitive instincts, that of destruction, whether it be of others or that of structures or indeed destruction of itself, *it,* the human would inevitably and eventually refuse to accept any such hands of help.

700 BC and Medea is residing on the Island of Colchis in the Mediterranean when to those tranquil shores come's Jason of Iolcus. Jason has invoked his birth right and laid claim to the throne of Iolcus now held by his father Aeson. Aeson's half-brother Pelias proclaims that he, Jason must first prove he is a worthy man to be king of these lands and Jason is sent on a quest to bring back the golden fleece of Colchis.

On first sight of Jason Medea falls deeply in love with him. Medea tells Jason that the quest he has been set is a perilous one and that without her help will almost certainly fail and lead to the loss of his and that of his men's lives. However, there is something that Medea wishes in return and that is for her help and on the successful completion of the quest Jason is to make her his bride. Jason agrees, it would seem that ambition was a great emotion within this young man, perhaps the greatest. And so, it was that they set about the quest and Medea led Jason to a large open field of grass and within were two huge black bulls the size of which no one had ever seen before, their horns were long and sharp and glistened in the bright early sun, their eyes were of a brilliant red and glowed. Medea reaches into a satchel and retrieves a pot of special grease that she had prepared and begins to smear this all over Jason, "how will this protect me from their horns" asks Jason, "it won't, but that is the least of your worries" replies Medea. On finishing Medea points to a Yoke that lays in the field and says, "your quest is to place that yoke upon the bulls and to plough this field."

Jason steps onto the field of battle and notices that the bulls are slow to move as he heads towards the yoke and he allows them to come closer. The closest of the two bull raises its head and snorts, two large fire balls shoot across the field and forces Jason to lay flat, the fire hits a nearby olive tree and because of its oil content the tree explodes and send three-foot shivers of wood in all directions. Jason now knows why he is wearing the Greasy cover. Jason jumps to his feet and grabs the yoke and for the next hour he chases the bulls avoiding both horns and nostrils and eventually he succeeds and once the beasts are harnessed, they become easy to control and soon the field is ploughed.

Medea then hands Jason a large bag of dragon's teeth and tells him to sow the field with them and once done he steps back to the on looking gathered men.

For a while nothing seemed to happen and then the very ground, they stood upon begins to rumble and move. No more than yards in front and as far as they could see clawed hands began to break the surface and soon before them stands an army of demons, fowl, ugly, snarling, snapping their fanged jaws and sniffing the air for prey. It is said that the eyes are the window to one's soul, but these foul creatures had no eyes just dark pits where once eyes were and thus, they had no soul. Medea shouts to the group, "if you value your lives, you will not move, but stand your ground," the men reluctantly and nervously shift their stance to that of readiness of war.

Medea walks to the front of the men unseen, unheard, for when she so wished Medea could be completely invisible to such demons and beast, this also included humans. Medea picks up a rock and casts it into the middle of the demons who startled by this at once begin to head towards the noise of its thud to the ground and there ensues an almighty battle so ferocious and violent amongst the demons that Jason and his men do indeed find it difficult at times to stand their ground with such violent carnage just inches from their faces.

Soon the dust settles as the last of these monsters are slayed, the field now covered in their black blood and Medea give's a warning, "do not touch this," for if they did, they would instantly transformed into one of those snarling beasts, but before the last of these words have left her lips there comes a cry from one of Jason's men for he has dipped a foot into one of these dark pools and now the very essence of these evil spirits are threading their way through his body, beneath his now translucent skin can be seen his veins now turning black as this scourge rises through his core. "Quick Jason" screams Medea, "take his head or you will all die," Jason does not hesitate and springs forward and at the same time draws his sword and with a single back hand swipe, he takes the man's head from his shoulders, his body now crumples to the ground and as it does it boils and melts and Medea orders Jason to clean his blade on the long grass.

Beyond the field Medea, Jason and his men find an olive grove of ancient trees and there hanging in one is the golden fleece. Jason go's to move forward to take the fleece but is held back by Medea as she nods towards a cave and laying in front is a massive sleeping guardian dragon, its tail curled about it, occasionally a puff of smoke coming from its snout, it had large brown dull scales the size of a warrior's shield. As Medea approaches the dragon raises one huge sleepy eye to her and stamps one large claw into the ground as if to give warning, she stands alongside, leans in and whispers something into the dragons ear, the dragon does not move but closes its eye and falls back to sleep and Medea strokes its cheek lovingly. On seeing this Jason springs forward and claims the fleece.

Jason was true to his word and on returning to Iolcus with the golden fleece he lays claim to the throne makes Medea his wife and she could not be happier, to then fall pregnant and to give Jason a daughter, life could not have been any the better for her. But not long after their daughter is born Jason tells Medea that he is to leave her for another woman and totally crushes and devastates Medea's seemingly idyllic world.

Jason wishes for Medea to leave the kingdom and to denounce any claims to the throne, she and her daughter were to become outcasts. Jason was to leave Medea for the princess Glauce, the daughter of king Creon of Thebes. Medea, crushed, leaves with little or no fuss, she knows that she has lost Jason and been disrespected and thus she's mocked and decides to try and preserve any dignity that she has left and simply go's to leave. The king Creon mulls over the coming union of Jason and his daughter and realises that not only would Jason be in line to his throne but so could any previous wife and child who may in time wish to lay claim to the crown and he wants nothing of the sort regardless of how tentative it may seem and orders his men to hunt down Medea and her daughter and kill them.

The king's men do indeed find Medea's daughter but not her and they savagely beat and murder the little girl. As dark falls Medea makes herself invisible and sneaks past the guard and into the dwelling that her and her daughter had been calling home, there she finds the tiny crumpled body, lifeless and limp and she scoops her up and holds her close and rocks to and fro.

Medea had the ability to bring a person back to life even those of great age but not one so smashed and broken. The first rays of light began to break, and Medea knows she must leave, she collects the soul and life spirit of her daughter and places them into a vessel and seals it. On leaving the house Medea is no longer cloaked with invisibility, she no longer cares. She walks directly to the guard who has now spun around with a look of total surprise, he recognizes her and is caught with such confusion that he knows not what to do, not even able to raise his spear. Medea grabs his tunic with her left hand and with her right she smoothly slid her dagger between his ribs and into his heart, she then violently drives the blade from left to right and cleaves his heart in two.

After much preparation, the castle and kingdom were now readied for the big day of Jason's and Glauce union. Glauce is in her chambers being attended to and fussed over by her many hand maidens, hair is teased into place and jewellery draped adorningly about the princesses' body as she and her maids laugh and sip fine wines. Then came the dress, delivered that morning from the royal seamstress to the gates of the castle by a cloaked and hooded hag of an old woman.

The dress was a beautiful white and ivory silk creation, tight fitting to show off the princesses youthful figure and with fine laced panels strategically place to be just a little daring whilst covering the lady's modesty.

Holding the dress aloft three maidens are stood on stools around the princess and they gently lower the dress into place about her. The princess stand's in front of the mirror to admire herself when the first scream comes, on turning she sees the maid who first touched the dress, wide eyed hands held out in front, these now melt and splattering onto the floor as if they were molten metal, more screams come from the other maids as the princess begins to smoulder and she now gives out a scream that fills the corridors of the castle. The king rushes to the chambers to find his daughter writhing and thrashing in pain, every movement another part of her body falling to the floor, her very flesh sizzling. The king tries to pull the dress from her body and as she collapses, he grabs her in his arms and immediately become consumed himself, by the time the royal guard arrives the king and his daughter have become one large boiling, bubbling mass of melted flesh upon the floor. Jason on hearing this news escaped the kingdom and it is he that goes into exile.

The grandfather of Medea, Helios the god of sun sends to Medea a golden chariot pulled by three enormous dragons, but these were no normal dragons such as the guardian of the fleece, these were war dragons, born and bred solely for combat, their ferociousness legendary, for these beautifully majestic but clinically lethal creatures could not be stopped once they had the scent of the prey within their fiery nostrils. Their skins were of jet-black shiny armour, there ran down their backs to a scythe like tail a ridge of razor-sharp scales, two large horns adorned their heads with further smaller horns that ran down the sides of their face to a jaw that held a thousand tall, serrated teeth, brilliant glowing red eyes were sunk into the skull. They grabbed and clawed at the air, straining at their reigns to be let loose, for they knew what their purpose was, and they relished the task ahead.

On releasing the dragons, they dived time and time again snorting giant fire balls that would level entire buildings in one foul swoop and laid waste to all that stood. Once the decimation of the kingdom of Thebes and all its subjects was complete Medea Stood amongst the dead and smoking ruins and made this prophesy for the future,

"I shall put an end to this violent action of the human being from the lower level, and from this day forward will create a cult in which to do just that".

Some years later and a wandering Jason finds the wreck of his old ship the Argo, sat high and dry on a beach within a bay and sitting within the decaying hulk of its remains he reminisces of all the adventures that he once had in the vessel and decides that this is a fitting time and place to take his own life and throws a rope over the ships yard arm to hang himself with as he pulls on this rope to secure it the mast cracks and comes crashing down upon him and he is crushed to death, high up on a cliff above the bay the hooded and cloaked figure of Medea stands, and watches and after all these years and having had everything taken from her world, Medea took some satisfaction that she had not given Jason the pleasure of bringing about his own demise.

1646, Owlsden and Medea is still all seeing and all hearing and is fully aware of the relationship that has flourished between Louis and little Annie, she had been there the day they first kissed and had watched for months over their youthful and playful romance and saw no real harm in their blossoming love for one another. It was not however the view of the Count and he summons Louis to his chambers. "it has come to my attention Louis that you are having a dalliance with a maid in our service known as Annie Wright, is this correct" "yes Father, it is" "I should not have need to remind you my son just who you are, this girl is a servant in our employ, she is here to serve, so take what you will but remember, you are the son of the Lord of this manor and she is beneath you, have your fill if you so insist, but then be gone with her, for your destiny is that of a greater union, and that union is not here amongst these furrowed fields." Louis does not reply, for to do so would invoke the fury of his father, it was not as though his father had forbidden him from courting Annie, in a sense, there for he would just have to give the impression that it was just that, a casual affair, but that was becoming more and more difficult for Louis as for all his thoughts and indeed his entire being were becoming all consumed by Annie and his heart would skip at the very glimpse of the girl.

The passing of time in these parts of Suffolk was slow at best, but it would seem that the passing of time here In Owlsden was not dictated by any clock, but by the changing of season and one could tell what time of year it was by the crops growing in the fields or the lack of them. One could say that here in the village, time had in fact stopped altogether.

The routine continued as before, and Medea decided that little Annie had come of age and thus time to be shown one of the secrets of the manor, the tunnels. The wine cellar in the manor was brick in construction and because the manor itself was effectively sat upon water made for the perfect conditions to store fine wines, brandy and cognac's, but the cellar also contained a secret, and that was a hidden entrance to a tunnel, and in fact a system of tunnels. The furthest rack of bottles from the door stood about two feet away from the wall to enhance the circulation of air, just enough room to shuffle one's self behind and halfway along you would come to a patch of red brick work that to the casual observer had seemingly been repaired and repointed, with a firm push a two foot by two-foot section of staggered brick work would with the sound of brick grating on brick, would slide backwards and into darkness.

Little Annie was sworn to secrecy, "should I hear from anyone of this Annie, I shall know that it was you who has told of the secret tunnels and you will feel the wrath of me, do you hear Annie," said Medea, Annie not known for taking anything seriously did just that and solemnly promised on her mother and fathers life that she would never tell a soul, Medea could see Annie's sincerity. On closing the section of wall behind them they now stood in complete darkness, the kind of dark your eyes have trouble coming to terms with as they try to focus on anything but are unable as there simple is nothing there to see, not even a hand directly in front of your face. Annie at this point would have naturally panicked if it were not for Medea being here, who she knew would never let her come to any harm. Annie could hear that Medea was moving and with ease and obviously had no problem with the dark. There came the sound of a striking match and Annie could at last see a candle being lit, "stay where you are Annie" said Medea, the candle was placed into a recess in the wall and there then came a 'whoosh' of flame from the torch that Medea was now holding, and she blows the candle out. Annie took a moment to allow her eyes to adjust and into view came the tunnel. The tunnel was in stark contrast to the brick-built cellar, these walls were rock and roughly cut and the passage was about three-foot-wide, the ceiling had been rounded and was about five feet from top to floor which was also rock and felt a little slippery under foot.

The tunnels fanned out across the village from the manor to the church and a branch was said to go under the Inn, another section went to the brewery and the courthouse and on to the abattoir and it was said that there were tunnel entrances as far as the road leading south out of Bury St Edmunds hidden in some woods and that this was just one of many that were scattered far and wide within the region. But for now, Annie was content to be shown the tunnels within the immediate vicinity. Medea led the way and it seemed to Annie that Medea would be comfortable in these subterranean passages even without the aid of a torch such was her confidence in her movements. Medea came to a halt, there to their left the rock wall fell into darkness, it was another passage, Medea turned and pushed the torch into its mouth and the light reached some ten feet within and then faded, Medea then lowering the torch illuminated a sign that had been carved into the rock at this entrance, a circle formation of intertwined rings, "if you see this sign and any like it, do not enter here, do you hear Annie," Annie nodded, "Annie!" "yes, yes, I promise" said Annie.

They moved on and soon there came a natural glow of sunlight from the tunnel ahead and sure, enough there was the entrance leading out, it was covered by small trees and brush. Able to see quite clearly now, Medea shows Annie a rounded recess in the wall and she rolls the torch in this until it is extinguished and before she places it back into a bracket on the wall, she dips the cloth wrapped end of the torch into a bucket of tar that stands just to one side, as Annie observes all of this. They push through the undergrowth and Annie is surprised to find that they are between the courthouse and abattoir and just a short distance from the lane. Annie had become completely disoriented underground and it had felt they had walked a greater distance.

"Shall we stroll back to the manor in the sunshine?" said Medea and Annie smiled and nodded, as Annie looked back, she could see no trace of the tunnel entrance. "Annie" said Medea, "never use the tunnels without my Knowledge, do you understand," "yes, I won't," said Annie. But it would not long before Annie would betray Medea's trust.

Annie got word to Louis to meet her at the hay loft by the stables one evening. She had waited until dusk to slip out of her bedroom window of her parents cottage. She made her way across fields as opposed to taking the lane and found herself at the tunnel entrance by the abattoir. She pushed passed the brush and now stood in the semi darkness of the tunnel. Annie stood still and for the first time questioned as to whether she was doing the right thing, there was no question of seeing Louis, no it was whether she should now be using the tunnel, and the still darkness sent a shiver down her spine. She steels herself, lit a match and held it to the torch and it roared into life, and Annie felt a little better. Holding the torch as high as she could she began to walk deeper in and as she did it occurred to her that the path was also heading downwards.

As Annie gingerly walked on with one hand on the wall of the tunnel, she could see the torch light illuminating the way ahead inch by inch and as it did, so the darkness closed in behind her. Annie past the tunnel entrance that Medea had said not to go down, this now on her right, and made a note of the symbol carved in the rock. She tipped toed on, it became deeper and darker as she went. Suddenly from behind her came a shuffle, she froze, *what was that noise, was that behind*, she could not tell, she had become disoriented, she began to hold her breath so she could listen, again, did something just move, she swapped the torch into her right hand and without moving her feet, she could not with fear, she slowly turned at the waist and holding out the torch she pierced the dark behind and as she tried to look beyond her shaking hand, she struggled to make out anything but shadows. She held the pose for some time until a terrible thought creeped into her mind, *what if the noise had not come from behind, but from in front of her.* She turned her head slowly to look back along the tunnel but saw nothing but darkness, she slowly brought the torch back passed her face, the hair on her neck standing as she did, so began a slow low muffled scream under her breath, and there out of the darkness came..... nothing, there was nothing, but more shadows and Annie heaved a huge sigh of relief and as she moved on, her pace quickened, and it was with relief that she came upon the secret doorway that led to the cellar.

Annie stood still straining to hear if there was anyone on the other side of the wall in the cellar, she could not tell and so she had to take the risk and she pushed upon the wall and there came that grating sound again of brick on brick, she paused, head just inside, there was no one around and she quickly shuffled into the cellar and slowly close the secret door, Annie leant her head against the wall with relief as there was no way she wanted to go back down that tunnel again that night. With her air of confidence regained, Annie stood and went to head for the kitchen, as she passed the end of the wine rack she stopped, reversed and picking up a bottle of wine for which she had no knowledge of and thought, 'this will do nicely.' She sneaked into the kitchen and found in the pantry some bread and cheese and some linen in which to wrap these. She found some candles and made her way to the backdoor, dark had indeed descended, and thus, her cover secured as she darted out and into the yard and made her way to the stables and the hay loft.

Annie stepped quietly into the hay loft and whispered, "Louis," she paused, "Louis," she said again, had he not got her message, or had he not understood, just then Louis came out of nowhere and scooped her up in his arms and Annie squealed and the two of them fell into a pile of hay and giggled. "Wait" she cried, "you'll crush the bread" and Louis sat up as Annie unfolded the picnic and as she did so Louis picked up the wine and asked, "where did you get this?" "compliments of your father" she said, Louis knew that there was not a chance in hell his father would bless such a meeting, particularly with such a good bottle of his best French wine, "I got it from the cellar" said Annie, "and you my lady have impeccable taste" he said as he uncorked it; Annie liked him calling her *his* lady. They ate, they drank and talked late into the night, just the sound of an owl punctuating the still night air. Just as they both had their fill of wine Louis leans in and kisses Annie passionately and she kisses him back. "Louis, stand and take off your shirt for me," Louis a bit taken aback by this request but did as she had asked, he stood and as she watched he loosened the draw strings at the cuffs and then at the neck and the shirt fell open to the middle of his smooth hard chest, he untucked the shirt from his britches and then slowly pulled it over his head, the work on the farm had made him lean and muscular. "give me this" asks Annie and Louis tossed his shirt to her, holding this to her face she breathed in his scent, "well" she said to Louis who at this point had to be shaken from a trance, "turnabout good sir" and Louis obliged facing the other direction, as he stood, he could hear the rustle of clothes and hay and shortly came her voice, "you can turn now," Louis turned to find that Annie had undressed and put his shirt on, it somewhat drowned her but in a sensual way, coming up to just above her knees, the shirt had fallen open and one shoulder was completely exposed, her blonde curly hair hung down over one side of her beautiful face, all the time her curvy figure being back lit by the candles, she had her hands behind her, and her head tilted to one side, an alluring smile upon her lips, "do you find me pleasing sir?" she asked, Louis lunged forward and picked her off the floor with his strong arms and she went limp, head and arms hung lose, she had completely and unconditionally surrendered, she wanted him to take her and take her this instant. They fell into the hay, arms and legs wrapped around each other and without breaking their kiss Louis kicked off his boots as Annie undid his britches, she pushed him forcibly onto his back and she straddled him, and as they kissed, Annie still wearing his shirt, squirmed around on top of Louis until they both froze as he penetrated her and with a smile on her wet lips, she pushed down and hard until she had taken all of him, And as she rode and rived upon his body her hair swished from side to side and the shirt fell further down her arm and exposed one of her perfectly rounded breasts, their pace quickened, and they interlocked their fingers until a flurry of movement came, and they slowed, and Annie laid her head on Louis's chest as they both gasped for air and it was at that moment that Annie knew she was in love.

All fell quiet as the still coupled lovers held their embrace, the candles cast dancing shadows about the barn, all but for one dark deep corner, and from this black vale came slowly the features of the count as if he were emerging from a pool of blackness face first, candlelight dancing in his eyes a cruel and wicked smile upon his face.

The gallows dance

It was a Wednesday and like any other Wednesday, market day in Bury St Edmunds and anyone who had anything to do with farming would attend. These events were not all business and would be quite sociable, a market would spring up in the main square with all manner of stalls selling everything from linen, kitchen ware to food, the Inns were given special license to remain open all day and there would be all manner of street entertainment.

The count was here this day on business and was accompanied by Thomas, his main farm hand, and having conducted this business satisfactorily found himself in the main square contemplating as to whether to stop for a snifter before the ride back to the manor when he became aware of the gathering crowd. The count looked beyond to see what the attraction was, and there before him was the unmistakable wooden frame of the gallows. The structure was a wooden platform some twelve or so feet from the ground, held up by large sturdy wooden beams, stabilising beams were at each corner set at angles for further support. The platform was set at such a height not just to allow for a good view of the spectacle from all sides but it was necessary for there to be a good drop which in turn would bring about a clean and efficient snapping of the neck. On occasion, if the victim were slight in stature, a sack of wheat would be tied about their legs to offer extra weight at the bottom of the drop.

It had been necessary on some occasions that a person would have to hang upon a victim's legs after the drop because of the lack of weight and the victim would then suffer a long agonizing suffocation as their necks were stretched.

If the hangman had got his craft right, the drop and subsequent snapping of the victim's neck would lead to a quickish death, but regardless the bodies would go on for some time performing what had become known as the "Gallows dance" or the "dance of death."

The frame above the platform held four nooses. "Thomas, who is this for?" asked the count, "it's for witches my lord" said Thomas, Thomas had not the stomach for such a thing and seeing that the count was somewhat taken by this circus asked to be excused and the count waved him off and Thomas retreated to a nearby Inn that was now emptying of drunk's keen to eye the sport. The count found a vantage point and watched as a cart came into view carrying four women, their hands bound. They were led from the cart and up the stairs to the platform, some went quietly, some were engaged in prayer and one kicked and screamed her innocence.

There were two men on the platform, one tightening the nooses and placing hoods, the other was obviously in charge of the proceedings. Each woman was stood on a trapdoor, the man in charge gave instruction to the other man and one by one he would pull a pin that would release the trapdoor and that woman would drop to her death and begin her dance as the crowds cheered. The count stopped a man and asked who these executioners were? and the man replied, "that's Hopkins, the witch finder general." The count knew of witchcraft and the signs that would give a person away and the symbols that these people would leave, he had come across this in Spain and of recent he had come to notice symbols about the manor carved into the beams placed at doorways and above windows and it was not paranoia that at times he did feel he was being watched. The count stepped away to find Thomas and that snifter. Medea watched as the count crossed the cobbles and entered the Inn, she was dressed in a long black hooded cloak that went to the floor, the hood up, long wisps of white hair fell from within and because of this and her stance it was difficult to see her face, for she was hunched over, so much that a staff was needed to help her shuffle along, had the count glanced her way, he would have seen nothing but a wizened old hag.

Mathew Hopkins The Witch Finder General

opkins was born in 1620 in Great Wenham, his father was a strict clergyman and his family held title to land and tenements in Framlingham, *at the castle*.

As a young man Hopkins trained as a lawyer and thus had a certain knowledge and air of confidence about him when conducting himself in public, this enforced by the fine clothes he would wear, the very fashion of the day, direct from London. Hopkins outwardly gave one the very image, of an elegant, learned gentleman.

The sword that Hopkins carried had never been drawn in anger and was purely ornamental, part of the performance if you will. Despite he being the orchestrator of such cruel violence, Hopkins would shy away from any such situation if levied directly toward him, and why would he not, he employed Sterne to deal with such trespasses against him, for this was beneath a gentleman, such as he.

Early in Hopkins mundane legal career he hit upon a venture that would prove to be more lucrative, that of witchfinder. It was considered at the time that the scourge of witchcraft had become that of plague proportion and so severe that normal legal procedures would have to be suspended, after all it was impossible via continental or roman law to gain a confession from the devil himself, so confessions would have to be gleaned from his disciples, the witches, and gleaned in any way seen fit. Hopkins drew up false papers that to an unknowing eye would seem to proclaim him as witchfinder general and that he was blessed by the church for this task and in the service of the British government and crown.

Because of the civil war, it would be some time before Hopkins and his crusade would come to the attention of parliament, by which time Hopkins and his henchmen had murdered more than three hundred people most of which were women that hailed from the counties of East Anglia, most, if not all, perfectly innocent.

Hopkins had in his employment a small gang of crones led by his henchman John Stearne. The crones would be sent ahead to the next village or town on their tour, were they would infiltrate the local community and gleam information on potential victims, in these times, a seemingly casual overheard comment wishing your neighbour ill would be grounds to be investigated. Should no information be forthcoming? concerning a community, the crones would simply begin to spread rumours and whip up fervour. By the time Hopkins came to town the, scene was set, he would approach the local authorities and convince them that they had a problem and for a price he would eradicate such problems and cleanse the parish and thus save their souls from the devil himself, and for taking on such a perilous task, Hopkins would humbly ask for a purse of only twenty shillings.

John Stearne hailed from Long Melford Suffolk and was quite a bit older than Hopkins. Sterne was tasked with the everyday running of the operation, the organisation of the crones, the transportation and erection of gallows and the rounding up of the suspected witches. But there was another part that Sterne did play, one for which he did relish and brought to the performance an enthusiasm as good as any actor of the day, that of 'pricker'. Pricking was a method of proving beyond all doubt, having exhausted all evidence, that the person stood in the dock before all was indeed a witch. On the instruction of Hopkins, Sterne would reveal the 'needle' to the captivated on looking crowd. The needle was a long, wooden thin stake that was blunt and rounded at one end and the other end would be needle like, Sterne allowing people in the front row to press a finger upon it. What would then unfold and with great theatrics, Sterne would have the accused held whilst he would roll up her sleeve and taking the needle would drive this into her arm, if she reacted with pain and her skin was broken and she did indeed bleed, then she was a mere mortal, innocent and would be set free. However, what would actually happen, is Sterne using sleight of hand at a given point would spin the needle so, the sharpened end was now up his sleeve and with great enthusiasm he would set about trying to drive the now blunt end into the accused arm only to reel away, revealing perfectly unharmed skin and just to reinforce this he would then to a gasping audience present the re-spun needle, it's point free from any blood, "and so, good people, *we* have a witch," Hopkins would pronounce.

In an attempt to alleviate the shear boredom that had now engulfed him, and to but try to elevate his fitness and gain back his skill at arms, the count has taken to the stable yard where he has filled some nets with hay and has strategically place these about the yard at differing heights. He strips to his waist now only wearing knee high boots and leather britches he warms up, using his sword, he bends, stretches and twists for some time. He then stands to attention in the centre of the yard, still, statuesque, he salutes an imaginary foe and there then begins a carefully choreographed performance of swordsmanship, every toe and every heal is placed just so as he lunges and pirouettes, sometimes he defends and sometimes he goes on the attack, the razor sharp blade cutting through the air with a zip and a zing that would scream at anyone to keep their distance. He makes short work of the hay nets that now lay in tatters and on hearing the approach of someone he positions himself so at the point they round the corner the count is there, sword outstretched ready to parry the unseen attacker, as Annie comes into view, she is met with a swords tip that is now making a zinging sound, no more than inches from her face and she freezes with terror. It's the first time the count has laid eyes upon Annie since her late- night hay loft rendezvous with his son and he is now running his eyes over her as if she is again naked recounting the scene in his mind. A long lock of Annie's golden hair is now across her face and the count gently pick's this up with the tip of his blade and moves it back to the side of Annie's cheek. "what brings you here girl," "I'm on and errand for mistress Medea" replied Annie unable to take her eyes from the sword. The count flattens the blade against Annie's cheek and then runs it down her neck, the vain beneath pulsating, he allows the blade to drop and it come to rest upon her pronounced collar bone, following this line to her shoulder and he nudges her blouse slowly down to reveal just a little more flesh, he brings the tip along the top of her blouse until it come to rest at Annie's cleavage, and he makes a gentle tugging motion as if to try and defrock her. 'ANNIE!' comes a cry from the manor and it is Medea recalling Annie, she wastes no time, turns and runs as quickly as she can back towards the manor. The count chuckles to himself and resumes his vanquishing of an unseen enemy in his ballet of combat, his very own dance of death.

For a good while Medea manages to keep Annie from harm's way but inevitably Annie and the count were to cross paths once again. It was a bright summer day and Annie had been sent to the abattoir to collect some meat. As Annie stood by the side of the lane basket in hand there came down the hill a Gig, a small two-person carriage being pulled by a horse. Annie recognised the two people aboard immediately as the count and his wife Kathrine. The count came to a holt beside Annie and asks as to what she was doing? Annie curtsies and tells the count that she had been ask by Medea to fetch some meat for that evening meal at the manor. The count grunts and goes to pull away when he is stopped by Kathrine, "can we not bring the girl with us?" she asks, "no!" said the count, "but why not husband, we are on our way to the manor?" "Kathrine she is a servant, let her serve," was the response, Annie smiles and curtsies to Kathrine and scowls at the count as he slaps the reigns and they pull away. A mischievous smile comes upon Annie's face and she turns and runs, as the count looks back Annie is no longer to be seen. Annie dives into the tunnel and soon she is surfacing in the manor and stood upon the front steps as the count and his wife trots into the forecourt, the look of bewilderment upon the counts face is in stark contrast to the smug look on Annie's.

The count having become somewhat suspicious of what was occurring within his own household was now ever more vigilant of the day to day coming and goings of all about him. The count was looking down on the rear courtyard leading from the kitchen when he spies a meeting between Medea and Annie and although he cannot hear what is being said he can read their mannerism's. From what starts as a seemingly normal conversation, the count soon realises that Medea is now talking of Annie's wellbeing, Medea go's from holding Annie's face to placing her hands upon her stomach and they then hug. The count reels back into the room, and says to himself out loud, "that stupid son of mind has fathered a child."

Over the coming weeks the count became a recluse only emerging from his quarters with arms full of paperwork or with letters to be sent via Newmarket and would occasionally be seen walking the courthouse grounds. The count then engaged three of his men from the farm, two builders and a labourer. They set about clearing out the bottom of the pond that was fifteen feet from the side door of the courthouse. They then began to dig the trenches, first one long trench from the pond that ran down the sloped garden to a further pond that was not far from the brewery. A shorter trench is then dug from the end of the first pond back past the courthouse door towards the lane and the stream. The workmen wait for two to three days of good weather and they construct in the now dammed stream bottom a brick box that is about three feet by three feet and stands about three feet tall. If standing in the lane and looking at the courthouse,

the first sluice gate is built into the left wall of the box and is of a solid oak Finish with iron straps and rivets, and this when closed would halt the stream in its tracks. Into the back wall of the box, the wall closest to the courthouse a second sluice gate is built, same construction as the first. The dammed stream is now released to continue to follow through the open first sluice.

With the second sluice closed and holding back the water the three men now brick line the trench back towards the pond. The walls are about three-foot-high, and the channel is about two foot wide. On reaching the pond a third sluice is constructed and then a fourth sluice is constructed at the side of the pond in the mouth of the channel that leads down to the overflow pond and that channel is again brick lined. All the time the three men debate as to what the count could possibly want with such an irrigation system as the courthouse gardens held no crops and no fruit trees just the normal array, and a curious old gnarled oak by the pond, but what of it, who were they to question the wisdom of the count, they were being paid good money and that's all that mattered.

The count summons his son once again and this time the boy's mother, Kathrine is present. "come in my son" Louis was in work cloths having come directly from helping Thomas on the farm, "good day mama" says Louis as he enters and sits. "My son your father informs me that you are having a dalliance with one of our servant's a maid by the name of Annie Wright, is this correct?" "yes mama," "and how long has this been so" she asks of him as she looks at her husband with a quizzical expression, the count now pacing the floor hands behind his back, "for some three seasons now mama," again Kathrine looks at her husband but this time with distain, her attention now falls back onto Louis, "Louis my son, your father and I have gone to lengths concerning your education and upbringing, I have even overlooked your consistent persistence in dirtying one's hands with matters of the land, and have thought this, would, if nothing, keep one strong and agile if not mentally stimulated," she sighs, "and trust me my son I for one, know all too well that there is so precious little else to do here, but this" Kathrine ends the sentence by raising her voice slightly, "but mama," Louis tries to interrupt her, but is silenced with a wave of Kathrine's hand. "No! Louis, you are destined to marry into the royal courts of Europe, our house is shortly to rejoice in such a union, a union for which shall be fitting to our station, you are Louis to take a hand of a princess of good standing, one from such a household that will triumphantly announce our long overdue return to such salubrious circles, do you hear me my son" Kathrine shouts as she stands. "but we are in love" cries Louis, the count now unable to take any more of his wife's shrill like squawks of frustration launches forward and takes his son clean off of his chair by clasping him by his jaw, standing him up on his toes he propels Louis backwards at high speed and slams his back into the wood panelling of the wall behind, the count leans into Louis's ear and hisses, "you shall desist in the pursuit of this peasant girl instantly, do you hear", Louis does not respond but tears have welled up in his eyes as the count allows his body to slide back down the wall and his heels to make contact with the floor once again. Louis now shaken and without word scrambles from the room, slamming the door as he leaves. "You do know that he has no intention of doing as we have asked, don't you, my husband" Kathrine comments snidely, "yessss" hisses the count still staring at the door, "then how pray do you intend to stop this," the count spins on his heels to look at his wife, and with an ugly twisted face that tells Kathrine that she is to pursue this no further, he snarls, "it shall be done."

Medea finds Annie in the linen closet folding freshly washed bed clothes, "hello Annie, how are you feeling?" "I'm feeling well mistress Medea," Medea takes up the corners of the sheet Annie is folding and begins to help and as the two come together Medea hands the corners to Annie and her hands drop onto Annie's tummy and she smiles, "is all well Mistress Medea," asks Annie, "yes, all is well Annie, with you and your daughter" she replies and Annie's face lights up.

The sound of horses hooves clattering on the cobbles of the stable yard brings Medea to a nearby window and as she watches the count gallops away down the lane, she wonders why he had not ordered one of the stable hands to saddle his horse and bring the mount to the manor, and where could he be going on such a day? there were no markets and she knew of no meetings.

The count was riding this day to a nearby village by the name of Hawkedon and to a meeting that he would rather keep from peoples prying eyes and inquisitive natures. Hawkedon was situated high upon a hill with commanding views of the surrounding countryside as far as the eye could see and thus anyone approaching and was just a few miles outside of Bury St Edmunds on the road heading south and it had but one Inn. The count dismounts and looks about him, he is wearing his customary black tunic, pantaloons, knee high boots, wide brim hat, long cape that held a lavish silk purple lining and beneath this the count was heavily armed, he had of late become quite suspicious of those about him and had taken to carrying weapons were ever he went. The count enters the Inn, of wood construction with low beamed ceilings, the air is thick with smoke from the fireplace. The Inn keeper acknowledges him as he pauses by the door for his eyesight to adjust. Scanning the room, the count spies a man sat at a table towards the back and assumes this is the man he has come to see. "what can I get you my lord" asks the Inn keeper as he approaches the count, "wine, I'll take some wine" replies the count and he moves toward the figure at the back. As he approaches, the man stands removes his hat bows and offers his hand, and says in a low voice, "I take it I am addressing Count Bourbonne," "you are sir and I gather you are the witch finder General," "yes, count I am indeed," a smile upon the witch finders face, similar to that upon the count but his, feigned with distain. Although the count had not the displeasure of the company of this man before, he had already a disliking for him, Hopkins, was dressed in the finery of the day, from his perfectly polished boots, pristine lace blouse, to the feathered plume that adorned his cavalier like broad hat. This man, Hopkins, although the taker of many lives was not the calibre of man the count would gladly take to battle, for the taking of a life in an honourable manner was about as far removed from Hopkins as the battlefield itself had been removed from the count in recent years. The men sit as the Inn keeper returns with the counts wine. "Thank you for replying to my correspondents says the count, "my pleasure, I understand you have a problem within your own household?" "that's correct" "a problem with one of your staff, a young serving girl is that right?" "yes, it is" "pray please elaborate count, I must have some of the facts surrounding the circumstance," "I have come to notice a number of signs that have appeared about the manor of late" "signs, would these be by windows and doors by chance?" Hopkins asks, "yes that's correct" replies the count, "please continue," "this serving wench I speak of did in front of my very own eyes and that of my wife's, disappear and then reappear a short while later" "that is indeed a cause for concern and would indicate a collaboration with the devil" Hopkins responds as he sits back to contemplate and takes a deep draw upon his pipe and says, "this I feel does indeed warrant an investigation" "an investigation to be conducted at the courthouse upon my manor," says the count "I cannot see a problem with this sir" "and I need the outcome to be that of a conclusive manner," the count leans in and says in a low voice, "what I mean sir is I require of you to rid me of this scourge, do we have an understanding sir?" "yes of course sir, I understand implicitly," replies Hopkins.

The count sits back pleased and picks up his glass and takes a sip of wine and winces at the taste and considers whether he should run the Inn keep through with his sword for serving him with such an insult of a wine. "I shall require the girl to dive" says the count, "ahh, now that may prove to be a problem" says Hopkins, "how so?" "well our parliament are most happy for me to rid these lands of the plague of witchery but now it would seem that they have grown a conscience when it does come to the dispatching of these wretches, for it has been deemed that I am no longer free to extract a confession by means of diving them under water, I give it to you sir, a simple test, if they are alive when brought up then they are indeed a witch and thus will be hanged and burnt at the stake" "and if they are dead?" asks the count, "well then, they are innocent to the relief of their families" "and do many die?" asks the count, "They all shall die!" replies Hopkins with an evil smile. "You shall have no problem with this Hopkins for after you have presided over the proceedings my men will conduct the execution," Hopkins nods agreeingly, "these are exceptional circumstance sir and I shall require reasonable recompense for my troubles" "I have no doubt Hopkins, and what shall that be" "ten-shilling sir" "for a good show Hopkins I am prepared to pay you the princely sum of thirteen" "you are most generous count Bourbonne" "I shall need to know the name of this girl" "why so" asks the count, "despite being despatched at your courthouse I shall enter her name on the registry at Bury upon that day, it will simplify the matter in a clerical sense, you understand?" "I see" replies the count, and he says "Annie Wright, the girls name is Annie Wright."

The Day of the Trial

The count and Kathrine arose early this morning for there was much to do. The count seeks out Thomas and informs him that there is business of a farming nature to be conducted in Bury, business for which the count is unable to devote his personal attention to, and so Thomas is to take the counts son Louis to act upon his behalf, Thomas obeys his masters wish and saddles both Louis's horse and his own before he in turn seeks out the lad and informs him of his father's orders.

There is to be a party this day, a gathering of local dignitaries and some acquaintances that Kathrine and the count have gathered about them over the years that they have lorded over these lands. Kathrine matter-of-factually informs Medea of the imminent impending festivities and as with any good housekeeper Medea immediately begins to give orders to her staff with calmed, controlled efficiency despite the underlying air of panic within them. Medea tells Annie to fetch a basket of meat from the abattoir that will be fresher than what is currently in the cold store as she knows that there was a slaughter only the day before, further orders are made of others to fetch supplies from the brewery with the use of the cart and Medea sets about dressing the great hall in readiness for their guests.

For others there is not such a necessity for the need to hurry themselves and Louis and Thomas casually walk their horses in the general direction of Bury taking in the sights of open fields of wheat and barley and the sounds of wildlife as the sun warms their faces. "Tis a good day Thomas for a ride out is it not?" observes Louis, "that it is master Louis" he then studies the sky and makes a prediction, "I'd put good money on it though, that we see a storm before this day is out master." "Thomas how long have you been married now?" Thomas looks at Louis with a surprised smile at the question, "for more years then I care to remember, master" "and how go's it?" asks Louis, Thomas now realising that the boy's enquiry was that of a serious nature responds, "it has gone well, master," a pause as Louis stares at Thomas quizzically, "she, the wife has stood by me master through thick and thin, put up with me when at times others of less a strength may have just walked away, she's done me proud, and I wouldn't have it any other way, why do you ask master?" "Thomas, I have a love" "yes I have heard" "you have? how so?" "we live in a small community master" "so you know of Annie Wright?" "who does not know of Annie Wright," Thomas says with a chuckle, "how do you mean Thomas?" "she is a lively one master, full of life, always was, even as a child" "yes Thomas and I am in love with her" "begging your pardon master but may I ask as to whether this be your first love?" "that it is Thomas" "then pardon me master but do you not wish to experience some, to travel, for you are a young man, master?" "no Thomas as you have said, your wife is the one, always was and always shall be and I wish the same for Annie and me," Thomas falls silent and ponders as he lights his pipe and the two men ride on into the sunshine.

Annie skips along the lane towards the abattoir basket in hand, she could not be happier with her life at present, she was in love and carrying a child as a result of that union and for once her life felt good and had begun to make sense. She collected the meat and poultry from the abattoir and began her return journey, down the lane by the courthouse Annie could see a figure but did not recognise this person, they were dressed in a long cape and wide brim hat that had been pulled down over their eyes. Annie walked on with a sense of urgency as the cook would want the meats back and in the kitchen as quickly as possible. As Annie approached the stranger at the courthouse, she made an attempt to say good day but again she could see no face and went back to daydreaming of Louis when all of a sudden Annie's world went black. John Stearne, the man in the cape had spun around as Annie had passed and had thrown a hessian sack over Annie's head and before she could react, he knocks the basket from her hands and it and meat is sent spinning across the mudded track, Stearne picks her up off of her feet and begins carrying her towards the courthouse. Annie's hands were tied, and she was placed in a back room and all went quiet.

A short while later and Annie can hear footsteps and muffled voices coming from the courtroom and not long after comes the sound of the bolt on the door being slammed back and the door open's and she is told to stand. Annie is then bundled into the court room, hands still tied behind her back and is stood in the dock as the hood is whipped from her head, the room is dimly lit, and she struggles for some time to focus on where she is and who's around her.

As her sight comes back to her, she begins to make out some of the people who are now gathered and seated in the pews lined up one behind the other to her left and some are people that Annie knows from the village and farm, some have ventured up onto the gallery and are now peering down upon her. There seated at the back was her mother and father, her mother was crying into a handkerchief head tilted down; in contrast her father was looking directly at her with a look of smug distain on his face. Workers and commoners sat in the pews on the left and the pews on the right were reserved for the count, Kathrine and a group of well-dressed people that Annie had never seen before. To their right a fire had been lit in a hearth at the centre of the floor which now crackled and to the right of this was a low raised platform that held a table and chairs, stood in front of this platform was the man who had abducted her, John Stearne.

Stearne still wearing cape and hat is now holding a staff, he startles Annie as he now bangs the staff three time slowly on the stone floor to call the collective audience to order. "pray silence for the witch finder general, Mathew Hopkins" Stearne announces loudly and the crowd go's quiet. In from the side door of the courthouse strides a figure dressed flamboyantly and takes up a seat at the platform table, removes his wide brim hat and lays it on the table beside him, he then takes his time opening a journal and preparing a quill before he looks up to acknowledge his audience.

"A good day to you my lords, ladies and gentlemen, all are welcome to this, the Owlsden courthouse," Hopkins looks at the count, "with your permission my lord," and the count nods his approval, Hopkins continues "we are gathered here on this day to preside over and make judgement concerning the conduct and behaviour of a young woman within your midst that has been accused of witchcraft, and indeed consorting with the devil himself," there comes the sharp intakes of breath and bewildered chatter from around the courthouse, "**order, order**" comes the cry from Stearne. Hopkins now turns in his seat to face Annie, "will thy confirm for the court that thou name is Annie Wright, and that thou reside within this village of Owlsden that doth dwell in the Kings parish of Bury St Edmunds England?"

Louis and Thomas tethered their horses in the market square of Bury and began to head for the corn exchange to conduct their business when Thomas begins to lag behind and by the time Louis has realised he is no longer beside him and on turning Thomas has now come to a complete holt, "Thomas what is wrong, do you ail my friend," Thomas had removed his hat which now he holds with both hands before him and hangs his head to the floor, he had words with his wife concerning this situation and indeed had words with himself, he was torn, his wife was on one hand right, 'what business was it of theirs,' and what if he were to be seen to go against the count wishes? why, it could mean the end of his employment and where was he to find work such as this. "I'm so sorry master Louis" "why so Thomas, come something is troubling you, pray tell" "It's your Annie master Louis" "what of her," anxiety in Louis's voice, "come Thomas, what is it?" Thomas blurts out, "the witch finder general is to bring trumped up charges against her Louis" "but I don't understand Thomas, what's this you say?" "they're to do for her Louis, to do for her!" Louis is stunned and shocked into silence, "Louis...., Louis, if you go now you can stop this madness, do you hear me boy," Louis is shocked back with a sense of the seriousness and realisation of the situation and he turns and sprints back towards the horses, "I'm so sorry Louis, I'm so sorry son!" Thomas shouts after him but he doubts he has heard such is the urgency in the boy. Louis reaches his horse and is upon its back in one leap and slapping the reins hard on either side of its flanks its hooves clattering and sliding as he hurtles across the cobbles of the marketplace sending traders and produce scattering in all directions to the shouts of their displeasure.

Annie still unable to fully comprehend what is happening to her, she can all but nod acknowledgement when asked her name by Hopkins. "The charge against you, Annie Wright, is on this day, the 6th day of August, the year of our lord 1647, is that of witchcraft, how do you plead, guilty or not guilty" there came from way off in the distance a deep prolonged roll of thunder and the courtroom dimmed into further darkness and stronger shadows grew from the fire light.

Until now Annie had been too confused and frightened to her core to begin to contemplate her predicament, but now she knew that she had to say something in her defence, and she blurts out, "Begging your pardon sir, but I know not of what you speak, I am but a humble servant girl in the employ of the count and his wife at the manor, I know of no witches nor have knowledge of any witchcraft, I am god fearing and the loving and loyal daughter to my parents"

Annie looks in the direction of her mother and father, her mother still weeping, her father with an air of enjoyment about him. "I am innocent sir, innocent!" she cry's as she looks back at Hopkins.

Annie had gone from the facade of lovable sassy, confident, cock sure young woman of the World, to a tiny Suffolk country village and a small vulnerable frightened and fragile child that she still truly was, her eyes now wide with utter fear, her shoulders shake uncontrollably.

The door at the back of the courtroom opens just wide enough to allow a shadowy figure to glide through and Medea sits at a far pew. "Your plea is duly noted, miss Wright," Hopkins announces to the court as he writes in his journal, he sits back, interlocks his fingers and proceeds. "It has been reported to me on good authority that within the household that you have confessed to be working in, that there has been a number of suspicious occurrences, comings and goings if you will, and namely the appearance of signs above apertures throughout the property, what say you", Anni looks puzzled, for if there were indeed signs, she had no knowledge of them, "I know nothing of this sir" she replies. There comes a flash of lightning that announces an approaching summer storm, it illuminates the entire court room for a prolonged second and Annie spots the only kindly face within, that of Medea. Rain begins to fall through the opening in the roof and onto the fire and there comes the crackling hiss from glowing hot embers as they are spat across the floor, accompanied by a crackle of hushed voices and a heavy sent of burning wood.

Hopkins slams the table with his fist and people's attention are refocused once again, "then pray miss Wright tell us of what you know of your ability to make yourself invisible," Annie does not answer as she knows not of what Hopkins refers to, "in this very lane miss Wright, you did vanish before the very eyes of people only to reappear moments later, and at some distance," Annie now comes to the realisation of what Hopkins is referring to and how that must now seem to the court, *the tunnels,* she think's and she looks at Medea. Medea is sat with hands clasped in front of her as if praying, she wished she could draw her dagger and kill every last person within this room this very moment, but she cannot, she cannot intervene for she has a sworn loyalty to her sister witches, to the coven, to the holdfast and what lays beneath.

Annie knows that in turn she cannot betray Medea and reveal the where abouts nor the existence of the tunnels and sadly returns her gaze to Hopkins without comment. Medea weeps for Annie as she did the night; she lost her own daughter for she knows what is about to befall little Annie Wright.

The hoofs of Louis's horse thud into earth banks on the sides of a hedge row that divides the fields. He had decided to go across country to save time, the horse now covered in white sweat, wide eyed and protesting with every slap of the reins, but Louis forces his steed on, for he must, on through woods, and stream and fields, on he charges with all haste toward Annie, toward saving the love of his life.

"Mr Stearne, if you will, please" says Hopkins and Stearne steps forward, and from under his cape Stearne produces a long thick wooden needle that's sharpened at one end and blunt the other. As Stearne walks past the captivated audients he holds up the needle for all to see.

The courthouse is now filling with heavy dense smoke from the fire, rain still falling upon it from above. Stearne walks to the back of the dock and behind Annie, her hands still tied, he rolls up one of the sleeves of her blouse and once again showing the stilled onlookers the sharpened needle and sets about the exaggerated act of driving this into Annie's arm, Annie shows no sign of discomfort nor pain only bemusement as she cannot see what Stearne is up to behind her. Once Stearne felt he had played out this act enough he withdraws the needle and exposed Annie's arm to the collective who now gasped in horror at the seemingly unscathed, and unblemished arm of Annie, and as Stearne uses sleight of hand once again to spin the needle back from blunt to sharp he walks away again holding up the unbloodied point of the needle for all to witness.

Hopkins eyes are drawn to the left of the dock, and into a part of the room that's dark and unused, there the smoke hangs heavy and thick and through this, as if a large black invisible bird had silently swooped, the smoke now swirls and curls into spirals, and there steps into view a translucent caped and hooded figure. Hopkins hears nothing but the deafening rush of blood into his ears, he cannot move anything but his eyes, he cannot speak but a low slow groan rumbles deep in his throat, he sees no face within this hood but now follows the line of sight of this apparition before him and it looks directly toward Annie, and Annie is staring directly back at this apparition, open mouthed. Hopkins now forces himself to turn to the court and see's that no other person is witnessing this phantom and he slams his hand down once again hard and shouts, "WITCH, guilty as charged, Stearne take her away", Stearne is shocked and somewhat annoyed at having his performance so abruptly curtailed, but he is also puzzled with his master for he would normally conclude the proceedings with a well-rehearsed closing speech, but Hopkins is now out of his seat and heading for the side door of the courthouse and with some urgency to his pace. The count follows and finds Hopkins standing under the willow trees close to the lane, "you obviously don't believe in prolonging an occasion Hopkins," said the count, as he approached, "prolonged or not you have your outcome count" "are you unwell Hopkins, for you look positively ill man" "I am as well as can be, physically" he added, The count pulls from his tunic a leather purse and hands it to Hopkins, "your thirteen pieces of silver witch finder," Hopkins takes the purse and tips his hat, "I take it you'll stay for the conclusion of your performance" "I shall not count, and with your permission shall take my leave of you" "yes of course, I think my men can see to the rest," says the count and with this Hopkins and Stearne mount and they leave with much haste.

The execution

The courtroom empties, dignitaries and guests of the counts take their seats at benches alongside the pond, hampers of light food are produced, and glasses of wine and port are served. The count stays standing as he takes charge over the scene and he is served a glass of wine upon a platter and as he sips this, he savers the scene and the moment. Commoners now file out and remain standing around the edge of the pond but on the far side to the counts guests, the two were not to mingle, but all shared one thing in common in that no one could not take their eyes from what lay at the bottom of the pond, there in the centre sat a stout heavy constructed wooden chair, at the ends of the arms were sturdy leather straps with large brass buckles to fasten hands, at the bottom of the legs were the same straps and buckles. People's attention was taken away with the sight and sound of Annie being dragged from the courthouse, there was a man on each arm and despite the slightness of Annie they were struggling to walk her to the pond as she dug her heals in and fought back against them, they, the men now regretting removing the rope from her wrists.

Annie was protesting her innocence all the way, "why are you doing this, I am no witch," the closer they managed to get her to the pond the more sorrowful her pleas became, "please! please! I beg of you, please sir," she directs at the count as they pass, "please do not do this to me, I am innocent, please hear me I beseech thy, please!" she cry's, Annie's mother is inconsolable stood at the pond side, something that could not be said of some, who had come to relish such a curiosity as this, cruel smiles upon the fool's faces. Medea is struck with utter disbelief at the unfolding scene and that of complete hopelessness at her inability to intervene, she had killed in less a situation and kill better people than this and yet she can do nothing.

Annie is now reduced to uncontrolled sobbing as she is placed into the chair and the men buckle the straps at her ankles and do the same at her wrists. With the stage set the count now takes charge of this orchestrated performance and becomes conductor of his machine of torture and death.

The count stands poised before his audience and with a wave of his hand directs his men to open the sluice gate at the pond edge and the water rushes in under pressure and soon begins to fill the pond, the water soon rises up Annie's legs and spills into her laps and she screams "nooooo! please no", on the water comes and quickly reaches her chest and Annie instinctively throws her head back against the chair and stretches her neck as far as she can, desperately trying to keep her mouth clear of the cold stream water, her screams are snuffed out in an instant as the water quickly flows over the top of her head and there comes an eerie silence, the count orders the sluice gate to be shut fast to holt the flow of water and he waits, his two henchmen move to the sluice gate at the side of the pond, its channel leading to the overflow pond further down the slope of the courthouse grounds. The two men wait nervously with anticipation for the next order from the count, and again he waits for what seems like a lifetime, for the count has become distracted by what looks like to him a figure floating beneath the water just in front of Annie and it's not until one of his henchmen mutters, "my lord" that the count is snapped back to the here and now and he drags his eyes from the vision and looking in the direction of his men and simply nods at them to open the gate and release the water, on returning his sight to the bottom of the pond, whatever elusion there had been was now gone.

The pond empties quickly and as the level falls and Annie's face is exposed the sounds of her cries and sputters again fills the air, the gate is closed, and the henchmen return to the stream sluice and begin filling the first channel to repeat the whole process. The count squats by the pond and makes eye contact with Annie who is coughing up water and gasping for air, "Annie Wright are you now ready to admit that you are a witch" "no never! I am not a witch, I am innocent of these charges, innocent!" Annie defiantly screams back, "save yourself child and confess your pact with the devil, if not for you, for the sake of your family," nonchalantly responds the count, "NEVER!" comes the cry from Annie, the count stands and faces his guests, arms raised and with a look that says, 'we have but tried, have we not,' his guests now thoroughly enjoying the show and of course the copious amounts of free food and wine.

The count turns to his men who are now stood at the sluice by the stream having refilled the channel leading to the pond, they have their hats in hand and with a look about them that initially tells the count that something has gone very wrong with his splendid killing device. The count strides purposefully towards them with an expression of annoyance on his face which turns to that of share delight on reaching the channel. The count turns and strides back to his little social gathering and with arms outstretched, glass still in hand he gleefully pronounces. "did I not promise you a spectacle, then witness!" he gestures for the gate at the pond to be opened and his two men look at each other with hesitation before they reluctantly comply for the channel is now full of blood, guts and entrails that have been washed downstream from the abattoir and the slaughter of the day before. Unlike before when the gate was opened and the water eagerly rushed in, this time the heavily blood laden crimson tide now oozes into the pond with the consistency of warm honey, and as it creeps and swirls about Annie's body some onlookers reel away either from this deeply unsettling sight, that and from the heavily overwhelming stench of rotting flesh and congealing blood. Annie squirms and fights against her restraints as if these putrefying liquids were now burning the very skin from her body and her screams became sickeningly deafening. Onward and up, the heaving remains of these creatures now claw at her throat and Annie again slams her head back against the chair in a vain attempt at stopping this thick and heavy swill from entering her mouth, nose and eyes. Annie pushes head and mouth high, but she is unable to stop the inevitable and soon she is overrun, and this viscous tide of gore pours into her mouth as if filling a gurgling open drain and Annie is consumed, so consumed by the density of the blood that she disappears completely from view, much to the disappointment of the counts guests who had wished to see the girl's final gasps of life.

There comes silence as the pond settles and stills itself in an un-eerily quick manner, and from the centre there comes, slowly one large bubble of air that struggles to breach the surface and, finally, little Annie Wright is no more. The silence is broken by the sad wails of sorrow from Annie's mother and others and the cries of discomfort coming from the counts guests as they have to now fight and swish away a large swarm of fly's that have now descended upon them, this was enough to announce their departure and some congratulate the count for his entertainment as they climb aboard a waiting carriage, drinks still in hand. Medea orders the two henchmen to open the sluice gate that will empty the pond and this time it takes a little while longer but before it has, and as Annie's head and face reappears Medea is already knee deep in the pond and wiping the blood from Annie's face, it is of course all in-vain, for that wonderful spark of life has sadly departed, and Medea is left gently cradling Annie's face to her chest whilst she lays her cheek upon the top of her bloodied head and weeps.

She is joined by the now remorseful henchmen who go to unshackle Annie's hands and feet and one of them comments that the shackle of her right arm was undone, "how do you suppose she did that?" he mumbles.

Medea steps back as they carry Annie's body up and out of the pond, and she is laid out to one side, before an area that the men are to dig a shallow grave in. The crowd slowly departs with a seemingly less enthusiastic air about them, Medea sometime later returns carrying a thick mottled green bottle that has been corked and sealed with wax, just as the two henchmen have completed what is to be the final unmarked resting place of Annie here at the courthouse for little Annie's body will not be allowed to be buried at the church and thus, desecrate holy ground. From down the lane comes the frantic clatter of horse's hooves and Louis bursts out from under the weeping willows at the entrance from the lane to the courthouse and comes to a standstill as he takes in the scene. He rushes to the side of Annie and falls to his knees and gently scoops her lifeless body up into his arms and sobs uncontrollably.

Louis clears Annie's face of the blood matted hair and kisses her eyes and then her mouth, all the while saying "no, no, no!" softly beneath his breath. Medea kneels beside him and places a hand upon his back in an attempt to try and offer some form of comfort. Louis raises his face from Annie and looks at Medea and says, "but why, mistress Medea, why!" Medea leans in toward him and simply says, "she was with child, your daughter!" Louis freezes for a moment whilst he tries to take this information in and looks at Medea at first in disbelief and a sudden realisation come across him and he now understands everything that has happened and why. Louis kisses Annie one last time and gently lays her body back down and with a guttural scream direct from the pits of hell he stands, turns and runs back toward the lane and in the direction of the manor. Medea makes no attempt to stop him, why would she, how could she, for she knew of this pain, the pain that came from losing one's love, one's reason for life, purely as a result of another's twisted selfishness.

The henchmen lift Annie and walk her the short distance to the shallow grave and place her in and retreat with sorrowful looks upon their faces. Medea slides in beside her and arranges Annie's body so she is laid on her side, knees up, hands around her tummy, she could have been merely asleep from the look upon her face, Medea places the bottle at her shoulder, bends and kisses her one last time, retreats and a large flat slab is then gently lower in place to cover her and the grave is filled in. Medea sits for a while alone beneath the large old gnarled oak tree by the pond and stares at the now settling soil at her feet and the life that had been that now lays beneath, she stands and takes hold of a lower short branch of the oak and snaps this off, she then walks to the side of the pond and stabs this branch into the bank of the pond, and still holding this she recites this incantation,

"Apud haec peribitis autem vita, ego eorum hold vos, imperium vos, et quod haec

forti quercus non crescere, longus et fortis, ita eorum mea vindicta, apud omne

tempus cantium, vos eorum non morietur, Bourbonne, autem haec dies, neque

autem vos veni ut scio autem purgatorium, et autem eius infernales ita, autem

quia vos, Bourbonne, vos eorum semper quod, ibi clausus apud quod substantia

autem haec sacris arbor, ut flaccescere ego limbo puerorume, cit comeyh quod

dies, Bourbonne, quod dies autem bina et bina, et eius finalem dicens,"

"With this limb of life, I shall hold you, control you, and as this mighty oak does grow tall

and strong, so shall my vengeance with every season's song, you shall not die, Bourbonne, of

this day, nor will you come to know of purgatory, and of its hellish way, but for you,

Bourbonne, you shall always be, confined within the substance of this sacred tree, to languish

in limbo, til cometh the day, Bourbonne, the day of two's, and its final say."

Louis arrives out of breath to find his father entertaining his party in the grounds of the manor. As he turns the corner he shouts out "father," the count turns to face him with a grim expression, and he knows why his son is here. Without words Louis strides towards his father with nothing but hatred upon his face and as he does, he pulls his sword from its sheath with a zing.

The count casually puts down his glass and draws his own sword, to the delight and applause of his guests. The first few strikes from Louis are easily parried and deflected by the count and his guests begin to make wagers and light of the situation. The two men circle one another, "why father, why!" "you do not understand Louis, you refused to, so it was necessary," replies the count and whatever glimmer of understanding that may have been gleamed at this point is again, replaced in Louis with rage and he once again attacks. Through a flurry of blows, the two men come face to face holding one another's wrists and as they part there is a momentary lapse of concentration from the count and Louis kicks his father in the centre of his chest with the heal of his boot sending the count reeling to the floor. There comes laughter and cheers of "bravo young man," from the crowd as further wages are made and there comes a look of embarrassment and anger from the count, Louis's mistake is that he allows himself to freeze as he becomes briefly stunned at the vision of his father upon the floor, where as any fighter worth their salt would have finished him off where he lay instantly.

The count springs to his feet and there comes an air of seriousness about him, a sense of menace. There now comes a series of well-coordinated strikes from the count, fast, accurate and heavy and as Louis tries as he may to hold his father at bay, but it is to no avail, and it becomes obvious to the onlookers that the tide of this fight has turned, some would later comment that there was such a physical change in the count that they no longer recognised his face, Louis lunges forward in a frantic attempt to counter and again the two men come together and this time the scene becomes frozen as they are now again face to face. Louis slowly and silently falls backward as he slides off the blade which had been thrust clean through his heart all the way to the hilt of the count's sword. As Louis crumples to the floor the guests stand and applaud at such an unexpected extra addition to the day's entertainment. This appreciation is soon replaced by screams and gasps as they now see the vast amount of blood that now gushes from Louis's chest. Kathrine faints and is caught by the man standing beside her, others rush to Louis's aid but to no avail as his wounds are fatal and he takes his final breath. The count still stood sword in hand makes no attempt to help, there is a blank expression upon his face as if he were simply standing and gazing at an open field. Those who had attempted to help Louis now slowly move away from his body and away from the count who now turns and walks slowly back towards the manor.

The poisoned parchment

Medea rises early, before light and is accompanied and guided by an owl for she is soon scouring the nearby fields for ingredients, carefully placing them into a basket she is carrying, and by the time she arrives home the bottom of her dress is soaking wet from the early morning dew. She sets about preparing the ingredients with a mortar and pestle and bit by bit she adds these to a small bubbling cauldron hanging over the fire. Once cooled this liquid is then ladled into a large low dish and to this, she carefully lays a sheet of handmade paper and leaves to absorb the potion. After a while Medea retrieves the paper from the dish using wooden tongs and pins this to a line to dry overnight. She then takes a second piece of paper and on one side she coats with a thick layer of candle wax. The following day once dried Medea again using tongs retrieves the paper from the line and lays this upon the wax coated sheet on the table, she lines the floor with salt in a circle as to keep the spell within its source for to let it out but never back, two black candles are lit and placed on the east and south of the outer circle and sprinkled with blood of man. she takes a quill and careful not to touch the paper she begins to scribe and at the same time, she speaks this incantation.

On completion she folds the letter in the wax coated sheet and writes on the front an address, the letter is handed to the Inn keeper who will pass it on to the postmaster in Newmarket to then be delivered.

The funeral procession of carriages left the manor mid-morning on that day, the count and Kathrine rode together but did not speak, they had not spoken since the death of their son preferring to keep their distance at the manor, Kathrine remained within her quarters and the count took up residence in the lower rooms. There were few friends of the family that did attend, they dared not, it was mostly employees of the count and Kathrine who had come to pay their last respects, one of which was Thomas who had come to say goodbye to Louis, the lad he had almost come to look upon as a son. Thomas knew that to do so could be risky should the count put two and two together and realised that it was he would had informed Louis of the execution of Annie, but there was no connection made and in fact the count made no attempt to even acknowledge him, but then, the count made no attempt to acknowledge anyone that day.

The ceremony was short and once Louis had been lowered into the ground the gathered quickly moved away and soon the count was left by himself stood by the grave of his son, he had never experienced grief, all the people that had died around him over the years for which there had been many and most of which by his hands, had meant nothing to him. Here today he not only buried someone he knew, but his own flesh and blood, someone he'd loved, and for the first time in his life he was racked with guilt and remorse, but who would he tell, who would listen, let alone even care, so it was there on that day he did say sorry to a grave in an abandoned cemetery, a solitary owl high in a tree, for company.

From leaving the execution Hopkins rode directly home where upon he shut himself away behind a closed door, allowing no one to enter but his housekeeper. The housekeeper when asked later made comment of Hopkins behaviour, he was of course very drunk and did seem to be for most of that week but it was the conversations that Hopkins was having with himself, for there was no one else present, that most unnerved her, she said he had been arguing with himself and shouting, "it's real," and "they have come for me," and he had insisted that all doors and windows be barred and that besides her no one was to come near.

On the day of the 12th August 1647 the housekeeper had collected the mail from the town hall and let herself into Hopkins house where she found him in a drunken slumber, clothed in the same attire he had been all week and laid out in a chair by the fire that had long gone out, she set about her chores, lit a fire in the hearth and once completed she let herself out, once again making very sure she locked the door behind her. It was late evening before Hopkins came around and as he brings himself to stiffly stand, he again reached for a bottle of port that sat upon the mantle of the fire and takes a long draw of its contents. He staggers to his desk, still clutching the bottle and sits and lights a candle, he spy's the pile of mail and reaches for it, he discards to one side the correspondents that he recognizes until he comes to one that catches, his eye for he does not recognize the handwriting, and someone had taken the effort of closing it with wax, although there was no seal. He reaches for the letter opener; an ornate but very blunt bejewelled dagger and he proceeds to slice the paper open. He unfolds and now holds the letter before him and begins to read to himself, Hopkins is about halfway down the page and what is scribed here has taken his full attention and he has to pause to take the information in, he sits back and from a leather pouch he takes some tobacco and charges the bowl of his pipe gently pressing this into place with his thumb, he takes a tapper and secures a flame from the candle and begins to play this across the top of the tobacco and draws in two or three deep puffs, on exhaling, Hopkins experiences a sudden rush of blood to his head and feels quite giddy, he reaches for the port and again takes a long hard pull from it. Feeling slightly better he eagerly resumes reading the letter and soon he is totally consumed and wrapped up in its content, when he finishes, he sits back an expression of shock upon his face, he takes another draw from his pipe stands and still clutching the letter, he walks to the fireplace and throws the letter upon it and watches as it goes up in a flash of flame. Hopkins returns and sits once more at his desk.

He reaches forward and gropes for the letter opener, leans back and places the point of the dagger at the side of his neck, with great force he pushes the dagger through in front of the vertebrae of his neck and behind the large clump of carotid arteries and windpipe and as the point bursts through the other side he forces the blade down trapping these vital organs against the top of his breast plate and with the might of a man possessed he rips the entire front section of his neck wide open. Arterial spray covers the entire desk, slowly, his head rolls over the back of the chair, it now held only in place by exposed and expanding vertebrae and a thin ribbon of flesh, his neck opens up like a giant gaping mouth. Hopkins arms now fall by his side and the dagger is sent clattering across the floorboards some six feet away. Two brilliantly red fountains of blood now ascend into the air from either side of his neck, collapse and come crashing down upon the floor with a sound similar to someone throwing tankards of ale into the air and letting them fall. From the hole that once was his windpipe comes the sickening sound of gurgling as his body continues to try and suck air in and out, his body twitches and convulses, again comes the towers of blood from either side of his neck and again they slap and splash to the ground, the sound of sucking becomes frantic, his hands and fingers contorting beside him, again the blood spirts but this time they rise a little lower than before, the gurgling sounds lessens, the blood is now reducing to a steady flow; the shaking and twitching of his body now slows to an occasional spasm, there then comes a long slow gurgling exhale and all becomes still and quiet, and on this night the taking of innocent lives will cease to be, for on this night, Mathew Hopkins, the witch finder general becomes no more.

Across from Hopkins desk now dripping with blood there sits a window, through which can be seen an oak tree and sat upon one of its limbs are two owls who satisfied that they have just witnessed the demise of the witch finder now drop from the branch and silently glide away into the nights mist. The following morning and the housekeeper let's herself in and comes across this horrific scene of carnage and runs squealing nonstop all the way to the town hall where she struggles to explain her findings due to fear and her being out of breath, but the magistrate soon gets the gist of the scene she is trying to describe and soon the magistrate and his men are hurriedly making their way to Hopkins house. A flurry of activity soon slows as the group of men are now standing and looking at the remains of Hopkins and for some time not a word is spoken.

First man to move is the magistrate as he slowly walks around the desk and Hopkins, trying to avoid the vast pool of blood beneath him. He notes the murder weapon on the floor that was discarded by the assailant a few feet away and ponders as to why they did not take it with them, he looks back at his men and orders that they look for any sign of robbery and the men gingerly begin to tip toe around, the magistrate now standing at the side of Hopkins is overtaken by the stench coming from the corpse and flicks a handkerchief from his waist coat pocket and covers his mouth and nose as he lean's in close to examine the massive gaping wound in Hopkins neck, instantly out from the windpipe flies a large blue bottle and the magistrate reels back and gives out a small scream of fear and becomes instantly embarrassed as he knows all his men observed this, he barks an order to the man closest to the door, "get me the undertaker this instant" the man scurries off and he turns to another and says pointing at Hopkins, "when the undertaker arrives tell him to get that in the ground within the hour, is that understood" and he leaves.

The magistrate returns to the townhall and his desk and begins to fill out a death certificate for Hopkins, he knows it was murder and that there were probably a hundred men or more within the county that would gladly lay claim to such a deed preformed upon such a monster, there were some who would claim, quietly, that Hopkins himself was in fact in league with the devil and that his gang of cohorts were nothing more than a coven themselves, *live by the sword and thy shalt surely die by one,* but the magistrate could not have this as common knowledge for all to know so where the certificate asked for cause of death and after some thought and deliberation the magistrate scribes, *tuberculosis,* and thinks to himself, well, *the fellow did experience some trouble with his breathing, did he not?*

Medea enters the tunnel and lights a torch and is soon at the secret door to the cellar, she extinguishes the torch and silently slides herself in behind the wine rack and gently closes the concealed entrance behind her. On passing she reaches out and grabs a bottle of brandy and quietly makes her way up through the house in darkness until she comes to the door to the great hall where she knows she will find the count. She pushes open the door and enters, there sat in a large high back chair in front of the fire is the count, he has drunk himself into a stupor and is now fast asleep, so much so that she does not have to try too hard not to be heard. Medea stands and looks at him for a while and she has nothing but utter distain and contempt for this man, she pulls the cork from the bottle and begins to play the brandy over the legs of his pantaloons until they are soaked with the alcohol, she deliberately pours nothing of this above the count's waist for she wants not the alcohol to burn here but only his very flesh. Once she is satisfied that the counts legs are drenched she starts to step backwards slowly towards the fireplace allowing the brandy to fall and create a small stream, as she gets close, she, without taking her eyes from the count tosses the bottle into the fire and a ball of flames shoot up the chimney with a woosh.

Medea watches as the stream now plays and dances with a beautiful blue purple flame back towards the count, Medea has already made for the door as she hears a second woosh of flame, that of the count now going up in a ball of it. Medea makes her way back down through the manor, there is no need to be as stealthy as before and soon she is making her escape, again via the tunnel. The count comes too and at first, he is more bemused and curious as to why the fire seems to be so close, a feeling that is soon overtaken with the sheer panic and terror as he now realises that it's he himself that has become the fire. He jumps to his feet and franticly tries to pat out the flames, but all this achieves is to now turn both his hands into torches, he dashes to the door but it is held fast by some invisible force, it will not budge and so he now turns his attention to the large window but try as he may, he cannot turn the handles, for they too have frozen in place. Medea rises up from beneath the ground to a cool full moon lit summer's night, quiet, calm and still, she turns to look back at the manor some three hundred yards away and she watches as the fire takes hold of the entire lower floor, flame and moonlight now plays across Medea's face and from the depths of this inferno there comes the blood curdling screams of the count.

There was a heavy low haze of smoke that hung in the air like a vale that following morning as the sun broke over a sleepy Owlsden. Despite the early hour a good number of villages had gathered by the lane and were now stood, silently staring at the remains of the manor. The roof had collapsed as had all the floors leaving parts of the outer wall still standing, those giant oak beams now smouldering, pointing skyward, like the exposed ribs of some giant slain Neolithic creature. Kathrine had been in her quarters the night before and it was presumed she had perished in the flames along with her husband the count. Medea, who was also in the lane knew of the fate that had befallen the count but went along with everyone else's thought's that a terrible accident had occurred overnight. Medea gathered the villages, most of which were employees of the manor and farm and reassured them that their jobs were safe. Medea had over the years unrivalled access to the accounts and records of the farm and she knew that the farm produce was more than enough to sustain the work force and the needs of their families.

For many months nobody went near to the manor other than petty thieves looking for trinkets, and the odd bits of building material. There also began the expected rumours of ghost and spirits haunting the remains of the manor and people would not be seen anywhere near after dark, mothers told their children not to fish and most certainly never to swim in the moat in fear of monsters that lurked beneath, *if only they truly knew*, thought Medea, some even dare make mention that they believed little Annie Wright had come back from the grave to reap vengeance upon the count, something that seemed to unnerve Annie's father when ever mentioned, Medea was in fact very glad of the scare mongering as it indeed kept people away. But despite the ghost stories it did not take long before scavengers did come to call and pick at the skeletal remains for any plunder they could find. It was on one such windswept night that two such scoundrels did stalk and stagger amongst the shadows of the manor and begun to sift among the ashes: their courage spurred on by copious amounts of rum.

Robber one, "Ssssshhh, keep your noise down, what you trying to do, wake the dead,"

Robber two, "don't say such things, you know what lived here,"

"just keep it down and pass me that rum,"

"here take the bottle, I'm off for a leak."

One of the men wanders off into the dark as the other uncorks the bottle and as it makes a squeaking sound, he winces to himself and gives out a low quiet chuckle, "ghost," he says as he brings the bottle up to his mouth and takes a swig and as he throws his head back, he loses balance and his foot comes into contact with something that lays beneath the debris and foliage and as it clatters, he freezes for a second and his curiosity is pricked, he recorks the bottle placing it in his pocket and drops to his knees and begins fumbling in the dark and his skin is ripped as his hands become snagged on brambles only made worse as he pulls them back and he can feel his hands become wet with blood and it drips into the ashen soil. Soon his hands make contact with what made the noise, its long but light and despite the dark he recognises just what he has as he rips it from the undergrowth and holds it aloft, "a bloody sword, I've only gone and got me a sword," just then out from the darkness over on his left comes a noise of movement, he leans towards the shadows and says, "oi, oi," in a low hushed voice, just then his partner in crime appears to him on his right doing up his fly's and the first man jumps out of his skin, "what the bloody hell are you doing here?" the first robber asks,

"I was taking a leak over there, I told you,"

the first robber now looks back to his left to where he had heard the noise and squints into the dark, his concentration is broken as the second man now lunges forward and tries to grab hold of the sword and is handed the bottle instead.

"what's this,"

"I founds me a sword, look it's not even marked nor burnt,"

"that's going to bring *us* a good penny or two," the first was now preparing to make some remark about the use of the word 'us' when from over to their right comes a low long animal like growl sound and the two become statues. There in what remains of a doorway stands a shadowy figure of something, from the sound they would have guessed it to be an animal of sorts, but the silhouette was most definitely that of a man. There came a standoff, our two robbers unable to move, unwilling to breath as they sensed that whatever this was, it was in fact waiting for them to do just that, to move, like some stalking creature, it lay in wait for the smallest of reaction's before it would pounce. The first robber suddenly became aware that he had held his breath in for so long that his body was now starved of oxygen and with a huge exhale he now screams "RUN," both men crash and stumble back the way they had come in, through the under growth back towards the bridge, if they can make the bridge? they may be safe? they dare not look back for they can hear it thudding into the ground as it gains upon them, the second man in his panic drops the bottle and momentarily turns around and bends to scoop it up but from the corner of his eye he sees it, black and hunched, it is moving fast, and he could smell it, and it smelt of burnt human flesh, it had come so close by now he could feel it's heavy presence pressing upon him, he gives out a high shrill scream and again turns and runs for his life leaving the rum behind.

There was the bridge just in sight and they scramble for all they are worth, both men become relieved as they hear the sound that their boots are making go from gravel to the sound of wooden boards beneath their feet, "nearly there, nearly there" just a few more steps but having reached the other side they do not stop running until they reach the lane where they halt, bent in two and gasping for air, but not for long, for as they look back, they can just make out this shadowy beast now stood over where their bottle had fallen, they step off lively up the lane in the direction of the fox and hounds Inn. It was some time before the second man turns to the first and asks, "what was that?" "wolf, weren't it" said the first, "didn't look nor sound like any wolf I know," said the second, "look, not a word about this, do you hear" "why?" "because you dim wit, we've just been on that land thieving, that's why," nothing more was said between the two men until they reach the Inn. Now stood at the bar the Inn keeper brings to them two flagons of ale and wait's to be paid, the first man who is now bandaging his hand with a rag, gestures to the second with a nod of his head, who now reluctantly fumbles in his pockets for a penny. On returning the Inn keeper hands over some change to the second man and on seeing the first admiring the sword he has now produced from under his long coat ask's, "what you got there," "it's only a fancy sword, in it" he says, "let me take a look" asks the Inn keeper, the man, recoils with suspicion but then relents and hands it to him. The Inn keeper looks it over by lamp light and pulls the sword from its scabbard only to see the blade now covered with fresh blood and the Inn keeper then ask's "where did you get it?" It's ours, legit like" pipes up the second man, "yeah course it is" says the Inn keeper, he knows these two scallywags and what they were about, "I'll give you threepence for it" say the Inn keeper, "nah, more like six" say's the first man, "threepence and your ale for the rest of the night?" says the Inn keeper as he smiles, spits into his hand and offers it to be shook on a deal well done. And thus, is how the sword of count Bourbonne came to be hung above the bar in the Fox hounds Inn in Owlsden for centuries to come.

Life went back to its uneventful, slow relentless seasonal pace as it had for centuries in Owlsden, just as Medea wanted, the only notable event was that some years later a Lord Noseley and wife Lady Letitia brought up large swaths of land, some of which included land that had belonged to the count and set about constructing a large hall adjacent to the church using some of the material from the count's manor, most particularly the large French oak beams. Lord Noseley set about taking charge of the village and surrounding areas including supplying work to the villages and the wider community, he also set up projects for the good, such as education and welfare, all such acts going to prove just what kind of man he clearly was. Medea offered her services as mistress of the house and was swiftly engaged which was a for gone conclusion as lady Letitia, the lord's wife was in fact Lupia the fourth element of the coven. It was deemed by Medea that this time it would be more prudent to have more than just one of them close to whoever held sway over these lands. They need not have worried as it soon became apparent that Lord Noseley was not just a compassionate man with nothing, but good intent but he also could be trusted, for Lord Noseley did indeed know some of what his wife Letitia (Lupia) was, and what she was involved in, *the coven,* for he could also see the good that it did and the good it contained. But he was not allowed completely in, nor was he to know all, of the coven, for although he was indeed a good man, he was still a human. Lupia nevertheless, did indeed love the lord for the man he was and soon she bore him two up standing sons and so a calmness did fall upon the land of Owlsden and for a while all was good.

What lay beneath

Monday 22nd May 1995, Willow Cottage Owlsden Suffolk.

The now owner of Willow cottage a Mr Broomfield has engaged local builder Chris Carter to extend the back of the cottage and relocate the kitchen from the front and into this new section.

Over century's the cottage had been extended and modernised in all directions, when looking from the lane a section had been built to the right of the original courthouse and incorporated a (for then) modern kitchen, this extended backwards to form an L-shape in which a utility room was housed. In later years, the back of the courthouse was extended backwards to come level with the kitchen/utility construction, and both were taken up to form a new floor above.

This later addition was to become a living room and a lovely large inglenook fireplace built in a traditional way, it was during these later builds that some materials were reclaimed from Lord Noseley's Owlsden Hall, namely the French oak beams which had originally come from the counts manor. Over the years the Hall and the lord's family had succumbed to tragic events, Letitia (Lupia) the lord's wife was found dead one night in the grounds of the hall her limbs ripped from her half naked body as if she had been preyed upon by some massive wild beast. Shortly after lord Knowsley left the hall and took his two sons to London where they remained.

There were periodic visits from time to time, but the hall was all but abandoned by the family and in 1955 the hall was tragically burnt to the ground in a freakish accident.

Lance pulls onto a strip of grass verge on the lane outside of Willow cottage, it was just before 8:00am on a Monday morning. Lance stumbles from his car, he had stopped on his way at the local shop in Wicham and brought a pre-made sandwich, a packet of crisps, a chocolate bar and two cans of coke one of which he had drunk before he had gotten back into his car for although it was a good few hour since he had stopped drinking, he was not just badly hungover but still a little drunk, "I fucking hate Monday's" he says to himself.

Lance was in his mid-twenties, opinionated, owed nobody nothing, deserved everything but wouldn't give anyone anything for it, a 'hard man,' or so he thought, *he* had proper got this (life). He spots Terry's pickup truck and trailer parked in the lane on the other side of the drive, *why are old people always fucking early?* he says to himself, he walks down the drive, alongside the cottage and out to the back coke can in hand, "or rite, Tel, you old cunt, how was your weekend." Terry, although old to Lance wasn't in fact that old at all, he was in his late forties, he had been Chris's digger man for years, why? well Terry grafted, and he knew how to work a digger, that and he had a bit of respect about him for the job and also people in general. "Yeah wasn't bad, didn't do much, and you" said Terry, "usual, on the piss with the lads all weekend, went to the football yesterday, fucking useless," "you drinking downtown were you" ask's Terry, "yeah, we went into that new pub near the marketplace," "any good?" "it was alright until some twat got out of shape because I was looking at his misses legs, her skirt shouldn't have been that short Tel," Lance feigns shock, Terry smiles, "yeah, so I fucking sorts him right out in front of his girl friends," "good night then?" says Terry, "yeah, wasn't bad, at least I got her number," "who's?" asked Terry, "the girl with the fucking legs" says Lance, "always said, how much of a proper charmer you are Lance," a remark that seemed to sail straight over Lances head.

Just then the boss Chris comes around the corner and Lance jumps out of his skin, "I'm not paying you two to fuckers to stand around all fucking day, alright Terry, what's he fucking on about now? "morning Chris, you know, the usual, he took on the world single handed, shagged a couple of women and still had time to get a Chinese on the way home," "for fuck sake" says Chris. "Well," says the Chris, "well what," says Lance, "go and get some fucking lines and stakes out the van to mark out these fucking footings, for fuck sake, Lance!" shouts Chris, Lance scurry's off back to the front of the property. "so, Terry what do you think" says Chris as he nods at the ground, "should be alright Chris, can't see there being any problems as long as this rain holds off," "yeah, they say its ok till later, but listen, I've got the building inspector coming at the end of the week do you reckon you'll have it done," "yeah boss, no problem," says Terry, just then Lance reappears with spools of string and a couple of stakes, "mallet?" says Chris, "you what," says Lance, "mallet, you fucking muppet, how else is Terry supposed to put the fucking stakes in, with his head for fuck sake," Chris shouts and Lance scurry's off yet again, Chris looks at Terry and both men chuckle to themselves. "Right then Tel I'm working just up the road at the old slaughterhouse, any probs give us a call yeah," "I'll be back at first break for a sandwich, ok," Terry nods as Lance comes trotting back, large rubber mallet in hand, "if you hit yourself with that there wouldn't even be a fucking spark would there" says Chris to Lance and with that the boss leaves. Lance watches him go and on turning to Terry says, "I gather MAN U lost the weekend then, he's a fucking wanker that bloke," Terry raises his eyebrows and smiles to himself and says, "oi, bit of civility about you, yeah, he's our boss, now come on, let's get this done, 'hard man'."

About an hour and a half into the job and Terry had dug a trench some two-foot-wide, three-foot-deep and had come back from the corner of the cottage about six feet, Lance acting as Terry's eyes all the time. Terry was a very skilled digger driver: he could tell things about a trench purely from the feedback and feel in the control levers in the cab but it was also important to have someone with eyes on just in case they came across cabling or pipe work even if it was ancient, also there was an extra hazard, that of bombs, this area of Suffolk was riddled with second world war airfields and air crews during that time would often find themselves in a situation were on the return journey from a bombing raid having to jettison ordnance particularly if they had sustained damage and thus were at risk on landing. There had been numerous accounts of the odd bomb being dug up, some of which Terry had been involved in.

Just then there came the first muffled clunk from deep below and Terry immediately freezes, withdrew the bucket and swung it to one side, "pipe work?" shouts Lance, "nah it's not hollow, I'd have felt it, its stone of some sort, take a look Lance," Lance jumped into the trench with a spade and begins to clean up the edge's, Terry sits back makes a roll up and has a smoke.

Some ten minutes later Lance re appears from out the hole, "yep you were right It's a fuck off big bit of stone," Terry jumps down and goes to the front and peers into the trench, there laid in the bottom was a large thick grey slab of stone which seemed to be the width at least of the trench itself. "you know what that is don't yeah?" says Terry, "a slab of stone?" says Lance sarcastically, "no you prick, that's a slab of York stone" "and so?" says Lance, "that, my friend is £60 a square yard in anyone's book and perhaps more if we get it out whole" "fifty/fifty?" says Lance, "fuck off, seventy/thirty" says Terry, "but that's if we get it out hole," with renewed vigour Lance jumps back into the whole and begins to clean up the edge's further, the problem that they have is they don't want to extend the trench any further width wise than it was. With a cleaner more exposed edge Lance now directs Terry with quite precise hand signals so, the teeth of the bucket are now firmly hooked up and under the edge of the stone as far in as it can, satisfied Lance gives Terry the thumbs up and retreats a short distance, *you wouldn't want to be anywhere near if that thing were to come lose on lifting*, he thinks.

With deaf touch Terry gently begins to lift the large heavy stone and there comes a grating, rasping sound of metal on rock and slowly the stone begins to lift, as it starts to come clear Lance bends down at a distance to look beneath, Lance snaps up right, eyes wide and bulging and scream something at Terry who has seen this but is unable to hear what lance is shouting at him because of the noise of the digger. Lance without waiting for any response has now turned and run back towards the front of the house as fast as he can, "FUCK, IT'S A

BOMB" says Terry to himself, he quickly shuts of the engine and climbs down from the cab and gingerly walks to the front and bends cautiously in to see, "FUCK ME" he says out loud. Terry pulls his phone from his pocket, "Chris, Terry, you need to get down here mate, we've got ourselves a bit of a problem" and he hangs up. Within minutes Chris pulls up outside and spots Lance loitering in the lane, a pained expression on his face, Chris walks briskly to the rear of the property and is met by Terry, "what is it Tel?" Chris knew he wouldn't have got such a call from Terry if it wasn't really important, "and what's wrong with that soppy cunt in the lane? he looks like he's about to fucking cry" "take a look Chris", Chris bends and peers under the slab, "you are fucking kidding me Tel", and the two men stand and stare at each other speechless.

Chris pulls out his phone and calls the owner of Willow cottage a Mr Broomfield. "hello, Mr Broomfield Chris Carter, here, we've encountered a bit of a problem here Sir and I need you to come and have a look," Chris pauses, "yes, it is very, I appreciate you're at work, but this is going to effect the build badly Mr Broomfield," again he pauses, "ok see you shortly, thanks." "You ever seen anything like 'that' Terry", Terry shakes his head. Broomfield worked at the brewery in Bury St Edmunds some ten miles or so away and was able to get back during his lunch hour, if somewhat reluctantly. "This had better be good Mr Carter, I'm an extremely busy man" said Broomfield on his arrival, "it's hardly that" says Chris. The two men walk to the back and are met by Terry, Lance, had not yet ventured near. Chris gestures to the large slab still dangling in mid-air and the two men drop to their knees to take a look beneath, they withdraw and still on their knees Broomfield speaks first, "well it's a skeleton, isn't it? "yes, that it is" says Chris, "so what's the problem," ask's Broomfield, Chris a little bemused a Broomfield's lack of understanding and care takes a deep breath and says, "well this has to be reported to the police," "why does it, it's clear to everyone here isn't it that these are ancient bones is it not," says Broomfield, Chris now losing patience, "yes, they are old, granted, but it still needs to be

109

Reported," "then what," ask's Broomfield, "well the police will declare it a possible crime scene and close this off whilst they determine what's happened here" "and so" spits Broomfield, "well that could take up to six weeks or more," "I can't wait six weeks" says Broomfield, "oh its worse than that" says Chris, "I'm booked out for the rest of this year, I wouldn't be back until next year, if then," Broomfield for the first time now sees the gravity of the situation and he wanders off to think for a moment, he returns takes a twenty-pound note from his pocket and says, "take your men to the pub Chris for an early lunch and I'll take care of this," Chris hesitates for a moment, for he can see all the implications of this, "I insist" says Broomfield as he thrusts the money into Chris's hand. Chris reluctantly takes the money and gestures to Terry to follow him, they round up Lance still in the lane and jump into Chris's van. Broomfield rummages around in his garden shed and pulls out an old hessian sack and returns to the trench and crawls on his knees under the shadow of the large heavy slab, he had kicked up a little dust and as it settles, he see the remains of a human; he can't exactly tell whether it's a male or female but the skeleton is small, and, on its side, legs drawn up, he spots a bottle by its side and pushes this away, holding the sack open with one hand he first reaches for the scull and has difficulty in grasping it and has to put his fingers into the eye sockets to lift it and the act makes him shiver; he then begins to unceremoniously grab a hand full of bones and shoves them into the sack, he reaches for a bundle of ribs and sees a second tiny skull and is momentarily frozen with a feeling of fear and he wonders why someone would have placed the remains of a cat in here too, he is suddenly jolted from his thoughts for just then comes the rasping sound of the bucket's teeth as it begins to lose its grasp of the stone and Broomfield reels back away and stares up in horror as he realises just what's above his head, but he can't leave anything behind he has to get all of the remains out, so he ventures further into this gaping trap and continues to throw bundles of bone into the sack, he is just clearing the very last of this sad scene when there comes a huge and sudden crack of the stone coming lose and there's a slight pause before it begins to fall in slow motion like some giant slain tree.

Chris and the lads have settled into a couple of pints and a few games of, winner stays on pool, but it wasn't long before Chris was getting a bit edgy, he didn't like his guys standing around at the best of times particularly when he's paying, so it wasn't long before Chris says, "right, drink up we're off."

On returning to Willow Cottage Chris jumps out and heads directly to the back garden and on reaching the corner, he is stopped dead in his tracks with shock for he sees that the stone has collapsed into the ground and he shouts "shit" in fear and runs to the trench only to find that there is no Mr Broomfield pinned below and Chris is now visibly relieved. Terry who had followed closely behind now looks down at the slab that has broken into two pieces and says, "bollocks," Chris now turns and looks at Terry and says, "for fuck sake Tel," as if it were his fault and he stomp's off to find Broomfield. Terry walks to the open side of his digger and peers in puzzled as to how this could have happened, he thought that the bucket had enough of the slab in its grip that it was impossible for it to fall. Terry now studies the levers to see if anything technical had gone wrong, and on testing the lever that controlled the bucket he assesses that they are working fine, *so that leaves tampering*, he thinks and reacts quickly by first looking to his left, nothing, he now looks to his right and see's nobody, his gaze now settles on the large looming oak that is sat just behind the digger, its long-outstretched limb like branches over hanging the digger, its twig like fingers menacingly brushing the frame of his machine. Terry is held to the spot, mouth open, gazing at this wooden monster before he is jerked back to life and says to himself, *stop being ridiculous, it's a fucking tree*. Broomfield had indeed managed to dive out of the path of the falling slab but just before he does, there come's an overwhelming compulsive urge to momentarily go back and grab the bottle which he does only to come inches from the edge of this colossal weight as it thuds hard into the earth just inches from him, kicking up a cloud of dust, the digger rattles and bounces on being released from its burden and Broomfield has to wait until everything settles before he can assess as to whether he has in fact been injured.

Broomfield falls onto his back and exhales with relief, he now curses himself for going back for this bottle that's in his hand, how stupid of him he could have been killed and for what, he now stares at the old thick mottle green bottle and as he holds it to the light, he cannot see anything inside and again thinks how stupid he had been. He picks himself up and dusts himself down and heads for the back door of the cottage. On entering he places the bottle on the dining room table and heads up stairs. On reaching the landing Broomfield heads for a small door that leads to narrow low steep set of stairs that go up into the loft. Broomfield stumbles up these stairs dragging the bag of bones behind him, the loft is dim lit only a shaft of light coming from a small window at one gable end. The loft is a vast and open space and at an equal distance towards each end of the house sits two large red brick chimney breasts and it is to one of these that Broomfield heads with the sack. Broomfield had over the years come to know that at the back of one of these chimneys some of the bricks had come lose revealing a small cavity within, not exposed to the heat of the fire below it was perfectly safe to store things in and it was in here that Broomfield now places this sack of sorrow and seals it within by replaces the bricks.

You could be forgiven for thinking that the actions of this man were somewhat cold and careless and perhaps premeditated but it could also be said of Broomfield that perhaps he was predisposed of such a heartless character, this carelessness perhaps inherited from one of his ancestors who had previously lived and worked in the village many years before, the notorious Issac Broomfield.

The tale of two Spinsters

I n 1761 the village of Owlsden had a tailor by the name of Issac Broomfield, a husband of two wives and a father to more than sixteen children, no less.

In this year Isaac pursued and courted two spinsters in the village who both rather mysteriously died within two days of one another and of course, it came as no surprise that Isaac was the sole benefactor of both the spinster's estates, a considerable sum of money. There were of course questions asked namely by both the spinsters remaining families who were subsequently paid a goodly sum of money by Isaac to help, of course with their grief? at such a loss. So, although there were more than two hundred and thirty years between our two related character's, it would seem that the apple, on this occasion, did not fall too far from its tree.

And so, it came to be, that on this day, a day of two's, and after some three hundred and fifty years since little Annie Wright was committed to a cold, dark and shallow grave, her remains, and that of her unborn child were now interned within the very walls above the courthouse that tried and condemned her to a cruel and bloody death.

Home at last

Present day

Samantha and Emily crunched their way wearily through the stone on the drive of Willow cottage and come to a stop. Samantha switches off the engine of the Range Rover, lowers her head forward and rests it on the steering wheel and exhales deeply, they had just returned from a memorial service at St. Paul's Cathedral to commemorate the dead of the terrorist attack. It was a chance for some to say goodbye and for many to say thank you, particularly to the first responders, the paramedic's, the Police and fire service as well as the general public many of which lost their lives that day and for those who did not perhaps find a way to come to terms emotionally with their injuries both physical and mentally. BEEP, BEEP, comes from the lane and Samantha is startled back upright in her seat, its Rebecca the police officer who had been and absolute shoulder from the start, she had accompanied Samantha and Emily to London in which to keep the paparazzi at bay, as it would seem, Oliver, after many years of selflessly helping others had *now* become a hero. It was a lovely service, attended by relatives of the dead and injured, officials from all services, there were members of the Royal Family namely Charles and Camilla, it was deemed too risky for William and Kate to attend and Harry and Megan had problems of their own and of course there was the inevitable sprinkling of celebrities, it would seem that for this event, it was the hot ticket to have. Samantha had rather not attended in the first place; she could not think of many things she would rather have done that day then to put her personal grief on show to the world, one highlight of the day, a genuine glimmer was to meet Heather again, the nurse who had assisted Oliver at the attack and Samantha learnt for the first time that Heather was in fact still in training and Samantha was taken aback to think that she dealt with all that and she at the time hadn't even taken some ones blood, but

Heather wanted Sam to know that if it hadn't been for the direction and strength of Oliver that she may not have coped on that day. Samantha and Emily slip from the car and wearily make their way to the cottage. On entering Samantha closes and for once locks the door behind her something that she would never have done when they were at home but this act was symbolic, it was her way, after more than a month of being asked and told, being pushed and pulled, not able to grieve properly, she now, shut the world out. Sam turns to see that Joe had let herself in to check on Mr Darcy and had left two bottles of red on the central Island in the kitchen, *thanks Joe, you're a good friend*, she thinks. Emily is sat on one of the breakfast stools, elbows on the counter head in hands when Mr Darcy jumps up and head butts her in a show of affection. "You go and shower darling and I'll fix us some dinner," Sam says to Emily, and Emily drags herself up taking Mr Darcy under arm and says "come on you, you can't be up here" something she had said to Mr Darcy hundreds of times before and just like that *were things that easily back to normal?* she thinks. As Emily disappears up the stairs Sam spies a repeat prescription of Emily's sedatives that Joe must have collected for her as she cracks the cap of her chosen method of coping and pours herself a large glass of red wine and takes a big slurp, closes her eyes as she rolls her head back and heaves a massive sigh, "right dinner." Emily turns on the shower, strips and as she places her dark sombre clothes into the laundry basket, she wishes she were able to put them in the bin.

Emily awoke early the following morning, she had surprisingly slept well, not that she hadn't slept in weeks but she felt that had more to do with the drugs she was on, no she had slept and unbrokenly so, perhaps it was down to the fact that this was finally over, she pulled herself up sharp and said to herself *this isn't over, this will never be over, my Dad has gone, never to return*, but despite beating herself up she knows what she had meant, it had been more than a month since Oliver had been killed and it had been a strange month, it had almost felt as if she had been in a movie looking in, watching herself go through the motions and emotion being carried along, everything disconnected out of focus and somewhat dulled. Now Emily could at last take a deep breath, step back, start to take things at her pace and perhaps begin to finally say goodbye to her father but as she had thought just then, no matter what, it would never be a final goodbye and Oliver would never be far from her thoughts.

Emily falls upon her bed and pulls from beneath it a folder that has seen better days, but never the less, it is special, for this is no ordinary folder, for it contains all of her thoughts, her memories and for some years now it has been her sanctuary, a way for her to be able to try and but make sense of times in her life and although it didn't always bring answers, she always felt better whenever she had expressed her feelings within it. She pulls out a scrap piece of paper and writes.

I Miss You

Memories, even now begin to fade

Only days have passed but it seems a decade

Why has this been? What have I done?

To lose my sanctuary, my feelings of home where I belong

Nothing feels right

Never again will it be

Oh, to hold you again and you hold me

Stop this pain, my soul is broken in two

Please my Daddy let me one day be back with you.

Emily

Emily pulled on a well-worn hoodie, some shorts and slipped on a pair of Billabong flip flops, this was Emily's attire of choice her 'sloppy joes' if you will, even in the midst of winter you would always find Emily dressed just so, she had gotten into surfing a couple of years before and had loved it, the whole nature beach thing had really appealed to her and although it had taken most of those two years to get anywhere near good at it, she had loved every moment and to be honest although not massive nor gnarly there could on occasion be a reasonable wave up and around the shoulder of the north Norfolk coast.

Emily flipped up her hood and slowly made her way downstairs her limbs felt heavy and her joints where stiff it was as though she had been working out hard the day before. Emily said good morning to Mr Darcy and scanned the kitchen, last night's dishes where still in the sink and on the central island was the remains of one of the bottles of wine that Joe had left for Sam.

Her Mum was obviously still in bed nursing a hangover no doubt. Emily did the washing up, made some toast and honey and a tall glass of fresh orange juice and walked into the conservatory and watched the garden and birds as she ate, it was bright but there was a slight chill. Just then the phone rang, it was Sam's phone, and Emily moved to pick it up, Sam had no problems with Emily picking up for her, she had practically done it since she was a little girl when they were out on calls, in the middle of fields and Sam was dealing with the business end of a frisky horse, "hi Sam, how did it go?" "hi Joe, its Emily" "oh hi sweetheart, how you doing?" "I'm good thanks, Mum's not up yet" "she find the wine I left?" "yep" "good for her, listen tell her I call later, and we'll work something out about seeing each other, I think I'm going to need it if I'm to be quarantined with these three" "quarantined Joe? what do you mean" "you not seen the news?" "no" the prime ministers on, we're going into lock down sweetheart" "what?" "turn the telly on they'll explain far better than I, tell your Mum I'll call later, love you bye". Emily walked a little too quickly towards the living room before she realised that this morning her body wasn't responding to0 well, she found the controller behind a cushion and flicked on BBC one, there was the leader of our country explaining that we were only to go out for essential supplies and exercise for one hour each day outside of our homes, Emily was stunned, she knew of course of this virus that had initiated in the East and that it was quite serious but she hadn't realised just how serious it had become and just how isolated and closed off from the world she had become already, all through her choice since her father had died, *I guess I should be careful of what I wish for*, thought Emily.

It was closer to lunch before Sam surfaced from her bed, she was nursing a hangover from hell and slid delicately onto the breakfast bar stool at the island as Emily pushes a mug of black coffee, no sugar towards her which makes her shudder followed by a plate of dry toast, and two paracetamols, "did you sleep" asked Emily, "I guess, all be it alcohol induced" "I can see," says Emily looking at the remains of the bottle of wine, "yeah thanks Joe," says Sam, "oh she called" "yeah, she ok" "yeah Despite the lock down" "the what?" "The lockdown Mum, I'll let Joe explain, I said you'd call her back," and with that Emily disappears upstairs. Sam delicately tip toes her way through her breakfast and after a second cup of coffee starts to feel somewhat human again, she reaches for the phone hits a button and within a few rings Joes voice comes online. "Hello, you, how's your head?" "sore, but that was absolutely needed after yesterday, thanks darling" "the service how was it?" "as expected, Joe, just felt a little staged, you know" "yeah you said that when we spoke" "anyway Joe, I leave you for a day and the whole world is on its way to hell, in a cocked hat, what the bloody hells going on?" "yeah, I know, that covid 19 really did become a thing" "so we're not allowed out at all?" "looks like it, well it may be different for you Sam, you may be what they are calling an essential worker?" "sure ok, I'll get on to the HRA (Horseracing Regulatory Authority) and get the skinny direct from them, I am still going to get to see you, aren't I Joe?" "yes of course, I don't care what they say, I still need our Wednesday nights and even more so now that I'm about to be cooped up with this lot for god knows how long!" Joe was referring to her husband and two rather boisterous boys, "good well I'll let you go and I'm going to have a call around to see what's, what, speak later, bye, bye, bye and Sam hangs up. Sam makes the calls and as expected because she is a specialist equine vet, she is indeed an essential worker and is expected to attend emergency calls or to use her own discretion to assess each individual situation, *right, so as expected they have relinquished all responsibility and put the whole thing into her hands,* "fine," Sam calls all her clients and ensures them that if necessary, she will attend but for now all routine examinations are to be cancelled for the foreseeable future and rescheduled for a later date when more is known.

Dawn of the Dread

Day two of lock down and Emily arose early having again slept well which she had put down to the drugs she was taking, Mum was still in bed and she wouldn't disturb her, *let her sleep* she thought. After some breakfast Emily begins to scour the cupboards and fridge and it soon becomes apparent that there is literally nothing in, *what on earth have we been living on* she thinks. She writes a note to mum and leaves it on the central island to say that she'd gone for a shop in Bury, she then spends minutes trying to find the latest place her Mum had hidden the car keys, grabs them and becomes somewhat disconcerted and disgruntled to find the kitchen door is locked and is compelled to lock it behind her something that she had never known before. Emily takes the back road not knowing what to expect as far as traffic is concerned and is surprised to see some cars considering that they are on lock down but then she did not quite know what to expect. She chooses a large supermarket on the ring road as it would be easier to get in and out of surely and in fact parked quite easily. What strikes Emily first are the lines of people waiting to just entre the store, she grabs a trolley and joins the queue, a queue that is being marshalled and herded by staff to keep people two metres apart, it takes forty-five minutes for Emily to just reach the door. Some people are wearing masks and gloves and she now wishes she had thought of that and taken some out from her mother's stores in the back of the car.

It became clear that some items were deemed very necessary in the midst of a pandemic as there were gaping holes on some of the shelves where produce had once been, but somethings seemed none sensical such as the need for people to panic buy toilet rolls and it was becoming noticeably clear that the staff didn't have a complete grip of the situation as squabbles began to break out seemingly in every isle, this was bringing out the very worst in people, staff included.

But it was not until Emily turned a corner and came face to face with an elderly gentleman and he reeled backwards away from her in genuine fear that it all became just a little too much for her.

Emily quickly grabbed what she could and went to pay, again being ordered where to stand and even how to unpack the trolley onto the conveyer belt, it was clear some staff members were relishing their newfound power. Emily deliberately made no eye contact nor any attempt to speak either, she simply just wanted to get out of there and as quickly as she could.

On returning to the car she unpacks the shopping, returns the trolley jumps into the car, centrally locks all doors and sobs, face in hands. Emily had in her short life shopped on many occasions and thoroughly enjoyed it, in fact there was nothing nicer than strolling around a marketplace in a foreign country with all those wonderful sights smells and sounds, looking for strange and bizarre fresh produce to take back to wherever you were staying to then prepare that evenings culinary delight. But what she had just experienced was not just unpleasant, it was damn right frightening and somewhat degrading. Once Emily had managed to pull herself together enough to drive, she headed home and again on the back roads, if there was one thing she most certainly did not want right now, and that was to come across another human being, *never, would be too soon* she thought.

Emily pulled up in the drive of Willow Cottage and let out a long deep sigh, she opened the door and began to unload the bags of shopping on and around the kitchen floor when she was joined by her mum, "oh my word, you've been shopping, how lovely, you didn't need to go on your own, I was planning to go this afternoon, but hey thank you anyway, did you get some wine?" "yes, I got you a couple of bottles of that one you like" "oh great, thank you darling, and how was it in our new current state of 'big brother'?" "it was ok, you know, shopping" said Emily as she shrugs her shoulders, she wasn't about to tell her mother who wasn't in the best of minds at present just what an absolute nightmare that particular expedition had just been. Emily pondered for a moment whilst putting things away as to what she would do in future when it came to replenishing supplies, for the very thought of having to experience that again, filled her with dread. Since the call with Joe and Emily's return from the shops both her and Sam had pretty much kept the tv on for constant updates on the situation.

They had both attended a large gathering in London and according to the information they couldn't be sure whether they were free of the virus for around a further two weeks, but then again, the information coming out seemed scant and inconclusive at the best of times, but one thing for sure, they were both going to stay put until they could be certain. If the truth be known both Emily and Sam were glad of the isolation and over the next two weeks they fell quite easily into a routine of laying in, eating junk and watching utter rubbish on tv only punctuated by fleeting visits by Joe dropping off bottles of wine for Sam and the odd bits and pieces. So, it came as a bit of a surprise when the day came which signalled the end of their two weeks self-isolation and both were looking forward to getting out. Sam had been in touch with all her clients and thankfully there hadn't been any dramas concerning any of her horses, but then again, she hadn't expected any as her clients had vested interests in their steeds to the tune of millions.

Sam had organised over the coming week to pay courtesy visits to all clients not just to show a face but also to make sure they were prepared for what may be a considerable time period of inactiveness as far as racing was concerned bearing in mind the physical and mental wellbeing of these highly strung animals. Sam had asked Emily if she wanted to come along for the ride but she had declined as there was nothing, she would be able to do other than sit in the car and she wasn't quite sure if that was quite the done thing to do in present circumstance, nevertheless, Emily wasn't about to sit in and particularly as the weather had decided to perk up.

Emily wakes early and makes her usual breakfast of tea and toast and dons her usual attire all bar the flip flops and in place pulls on her old faithful well-worn walking boots, she leaves a note, says "see ya" to Mr Darcy and again reluctantly locks the kitchen door behind her and on reaching the end of the drive hesitates slightly before she steps into the lane. Emily turns right down the lane away from the village, although she was taking the bold step of venturing out she didn't really want to bump into anyone, you know, awkward questions, "how are you keeping, how are you and your mum doing?" she'd rather not and if the truth be known she didn't know how she was doing? she hadn't to date actually sat down with herself and asked herself that exact question. Emily blew out a large extended puff of air and emptied her lungs completely and then inhaled deeply, closed her eyes and was instantly filled with all the wonderful scent of spring and on opening her eyes she was greeted with the sight of a countryside coming to life. She had not been away that long, but she was having the feelings that an in-mate must have on their day of release or had she just been blind recently? Complacent perhaps? Emily strolled, this had nothing to do with exercise, she wanted merely to be able to put one foot in front of the other, breathe deeply, feel the sun on her face, listen to the birds and revisit the lanes and fields that her and her father once had. Emily turned the corner, passed the site of the old manor house and as soon as she could came off the lane and onto one of the many bridle paths and on seeing how tall the grasses and nettles had grown immediately wished she had put on a pair of joggers. Emily walked on, field after field, retracing their footsteps, pausing at places of interest in which her father had recounted tales of past events and there were of course those elevated vantage points where all of a sudden, the view opened up to give the most wonderful vista of a beautiful Suffolk countryside, rolling out below your feet for as far as the eye could see, and there she stopped, sat and willingly allowed time to stand still. She had no idea how long she had sat there and frankly didn't care, for the first time in weeks she felt a certain amount of contentment, not that all was well with her world, *that wasn't about to happen any day soon*, but she felt as though she was able to breathe, think perhaps, start to come to terms at the loss of her father, start to make sense, figure out how she was to begin to move forward. Some clouds had bubbled up over head and covered her in shade and Emily was nudged back into the here and now and had no idea how long she had been there, she pulls herself up and moves on to a patch of ground her father would always stop at as it was particularly rich with fossils and she could see him now, Oliver head down scouring clods of earth to come up excitedly clutching a piece of stone, fossil embedded, and with wide and wild eyes proclaim to Emily, "this is millions of years old Emily," to then spend the rest of the walk back pondering as to why it was here, what on earth had happen in this location to deposit such a thing, it just didn't make sense to him. On their return Emily would help him to clean the stones and they would take pride of place on a set of shelves opposite the fire in the living room and he had by now, quite a collection that he would always draw people's attention to whenever they visited. By the time Emily crunched her way back onto the drive of Willow Cottage Sam had already returned.

The next day began pretty much as the day before, and the day before that, in-fact Emily was beginning to forget exactly what day it was and even what week. Emily rolled out of bed in her t shirt and shorts, it was early she could tell by the light, but it had also become quite chilly, *typical British spring* she thought. She slipped on her flip flops and pulled on a hoodie, flipped up the hood and stumbled downstairs, there in the kitchen she spied a note, mum must have gone out early too, no doubt to see clients, she had to have left quietly and again she must have slept heavy as she was feeling groggy. There came the usual breakfast routine and Emily switched on the tv in the living room and sat on the sofa. The news reports had somehow become a daily addictive ritual. The virus was spreading fast and the death rate going up just as quickly, it was heart breaking and the whole time those 'on the front line' as they were calling it were pleading for supplies such as gloves, gowns and masks, it all seem like a really quite ridiculous bad horror movie. Just then from out of nowhere came the instantaneous snap of lightning so loud that it must have been directly overhead, and Emily jumped out of her skin and as she sat and adjusted her eyes from the flash there came the inevitable low long rumble and all went still, until from the front room there came three muffled deep thuds, boom, pause, boom, pause, boom, Emily's head span to that direction, "MUM", is that you? She had not heard the car on the drive and hadn't expected her back so soon. Emily got up from the sofa, slipped her hands into her sleeves as she was still feeling the chills of the morning and the thunder and lightning had done nothing to make her feel any cosier, she walked through to the front of the house quietly not knowing what she would find, she had definitely heard the thumps and they had most certainly come from within the house and the fact that there had been a pause between each thump would suggest that they had been deliberate, as she tip toed through she began to feel a heaviness about her, the atmosphere around her was physically changing, she could feel the pressure within her head building as she turned the corner into the oldest part of the house and she stood still in the doorway and scanned an empty room. The heavy oppressive, almost nauseating feeling that she had as she walked through was now suddenly replaced with a warm calming feeling of tranquillity as if someone had walked up from behind and slid their hands slowly around her arms and pulled her ever so gently in and held her close, the feeling was so calming that Emily closed her eyes and her whole demeaner physically slumped, BANG came another thump of thunder overhead and again Emily jumped out of her skin as she spun on the spot to see who had walked up behind her, "DAD!"

Sam returned later that day to find Emily with one of her father's jumpers draped over her shoulders, the arms across her front as if in an embrace. "hi darling, said Sam, what you been up to?" and before Emily could respond, "is that one of your fathers jumpers?" "yes, it is", says Emily, "what are you doing Emily?" asks Sam as she sniffs the air, and again before she could answer, "and have you sprayed some of his cologne on it?" "Mum he's here" "what are you talking about Emily?" "Dad, he's here, he put his arms around me earlier today" "Emily stop it please" "no Mum, I'm serious, dad is here I know he is" "Emily stop this, this instant, this is not going to be of any help to you at all, and by the way young lady just where did you get that jumper?" Emily looked sheepishly toward the floor, "from your wardrobe," "well I don't appreciate you helping yourself to mine or your fathers belongings, do you hear," before she could say much more, as if she hadn't said enough Emily at speed disappears upstairs to her room. Sam now left on her own in the kitchen covers her face with her hands and exhales deeply. Sam was now awash with emotions of her own, she hadn't ment to sound harsh, she was concerned about Emily's welfare particularly that of her mental state and up until just then she had thought Emily was *coping quite well, in fact come to think of it, up until just now she hadn't said nor displayed much in the way of emotions at all, so what was this all about, she's seeing her father now? and why her, he was my husband after all*, Sam felt instantly guilty and immediately pulled herself back from that particularly awful emotion of jealousy. Sam sat at the island reached for a glass and the bottle, poured some wine and took a large gulp, *so what's this all about?" she thought, she's seeing her father, ok, so what's this, some kind of emotional coping mechanism is it? is she struggling to come to terms? is she only now coming to terms? oh for Christ sake I don't know?* she was now saying to herself, *could it be the drugs? yes that could possibly be it, the drugs, I'll call Doctor Hendricks and ask him for his thoughts*, Sam picks up the phone and calls Joe. Sam and Emily spent the rest of day rolling around one another as if this two-meter social distancing now applied to them in their own home, it wasn't until the evening when they found themselves in the kitchen looking for food that Sam reached out and grabbed hold of Emily and pulled her close, Emily putting up no resistance and the two stood and held each other, finally Sam said, "I'm so sorry sweetheart, I guess this whole thing has started to get to me, I'm sorry" "its ok Mum, it's getting to us all" "I know, and you know what I also know" "what?" the two still holding on to one another, pulled apart, both tearful, "we're going to be ok, do you hear," Emily still tearful but now had a broad smile on her face, "and you my darling can do whatever needs to be, even wearing one of your fathers old jumpers" "yeah I guess I could have chosen one of his newer flashier one's," both were now laughing, "what do you say, I make you that pasta dish you like," said Sam and Emily nods with approval and the two set about pulling pots and pans from cupboards, Emily pauses for a moment, "Mum," Sam stops, "I do still feel him" "we both do darling and so we should and shall."

Sam was being called out to work more then she had expected, although there were no racing events being held anywhere the stud owners were still putting the stock through their paces and of course that ment there came the inevitable knocks and scrapes, so Emily would find that she was fending for herself more often than not which she didn't mind at all, she was able with the help of her tutors via an online presence to continue to study at home which she was now throwing herself into, this being punctuated by grabbing food or walks in the surrounding fields or simply sitting in the garden on good days with a book or her laptop.

It was on one of these breaks from studying in the garden that Emily had ventured into the kitchen to make a sandwich, cheese, ham and tomato with a side order of cheese and onion crisps to be devoured back in the garden when on passing the shelving in the living room where Oliver kept his collection of fossils Emily noticed that an old mottled green bottle was now laying on its side, Emily was unable to go any further with her impromptu picnic and as she placed it down on a low coffee table she curses at herself under her breath, *I'm not OCD, but I just can't leave that*, Emily picked up the bottle that was surprisingly heavy, she could see where it had stood because highlighted by a thin coating of dust was a perfect square where the bottle had stood, she carefully replaces the bottle taking care to place it back on the exact spot from where it came as she reminds herself once again, *no I'm definitely not OCD*. As Emily picks up her plate it strikes her that, *not only was that a heavy bottle to have just fallen like so, but she hadn't heard it fall either, anyway on with lunch, and then to complete that assignment*. Emily finished her assignment and felt quite pleased at its outcome, she placed her books on the grass beside her and laid back and closed her eyes and allowed her face to be warmed by the sun and her mind turned to the incident from earlier in the week, *had I felt my father's presence?" had he come over from the other side? and having done so, did he place his arms around me?* or was she just being utterly ridiculous, and all this was simply born from a yearning, a need for closure, a chance to say goodbye. She recalled an occasion when one of her tutors, a science teacher had been asked to take the religious studies class and he being a man, of science was of course open to all suggestions and influences and the conversation had soon turned to that of the paranormal and there then ensued a rather lively debate as to whether or not there was or wasn't such a thing. By class end it was generally being agreed that due to the wealth of unexplained evidence that it would be foolhardy to dismiss out of hand the possibilities of such a thing existing, much like the vehement denial some years ago that it was impossible for life to exist elsewhere in the universe.

All of a sudden Emily was feeling really tired, *these damned drugs,* she thought, something else struck her that since that day she supposedly felt her father's arms around her she had the overwhelming feeling that she was being watched and again a wave of *stop being ridiculous* washed over her, but she could not help it, it was there, and she felt it, *right a siesta it is*, she said to herself, *just for an hour and then I'll crack on.*

As Emily walked indoors, she became enveloped by the cool darkness that the low timbered ceiling offered and she felt a slight chill, she wearily climbed the wooden staircase that creaked and moaned with every step. As Emily's eyes came level with the heavy oak floorboards of the landing, she freezes to the step she had reached, for there illuminated by shafts of sunlight coming in through a nearby window were a dozen wet footprints all perfectly aligned. Emily steadied herself and slowly walked up the last few steps, her eye's now wide but in their tired state had not deceived her for there was indeed wet footprints as though someone had just stepped out of a shower and walked bare foot across the landing, "Mum, are you home?" she called, she then walked to a front window and peered down onto the drive, "no car" she walked back and stared at the prints. Emily kicked off one of her flip flops and placed her foot beside one of the perfectly formed prints and she could see instantly that these prints were neither made by her nor her mother as 'they' were both a size seven, she knew this from all the times she had gotten into trouble for 'borrowing' Mum's shoes, no, these prints came from a size six or less, Emily pushed her flip flop on again and knelt as she placed a finger into the nearest print not really knowing why or what to expect, it was wet, of course, she raises her hand up to smell her wet fingertips, and the water had no odour, Emily dashed back down the stairs and grabbed her phone and on returning she again stood and looked at the line of footprints and with one foot beside the nearest she took a snapshot; they had come from the stairs but there was no water on the stairs, she again took another shot of this. The prints headed not for a doorway or where a doorway had once been, *no* they went directly into a wall on the landing that formed the back of the fireplace of the master bedroom. Emily stood in the doorway of the master and glancing from the fireplace to the point where the footprints stopped, and she was able to confirm that the prints did indeed go directly into the back of this fireplace which had always been there ever since the house was first built, she took another shot of the prints seemingly disappearing into this wall. Emily moved back onto the landing and now began to tap along the wall to see if she could find any hollow point's or old doorways that may have been filled in, but as suspected, there was nothing, the wall was solid. Emily became even more confused than before as she headed to her bed, but she had at least got some evidence this time.

With the thought that she was unlikely to get any sleep now as she was somewhat hyped up, She flops onto her bed with the feeling that she may as well lay down and get some rest anyway and is surprised when she realises that she did indeed fall asleep and is somewhat startled back into consciousness as she hears the tires of a car crunch their way onto the drive, "Mum", and she leaps from her bed and bounds onto the landing only to have her rush of excited momentum halted in its tracks at the sight of dry clean floorboards with no trace of water let alone footprints.

Sam is hardly able to get through the kitchen door as she is greeted by an excitable Emily who is now bouncing around her just like a puppy pleased to see her return. Sam fights her way in and dumps her bags on the Island, "Emily…, Emily stop, you're making no sense, now take a deep breath and start again," Emily recount's the story of the footprints to her sceptical mother who had continued to unpack bags the whole time, allowing Emily's story to run its full course and eventually come to a stop, "you don't believe me do you," says Emily, "look darling" was all Sam was able to get out before Emily says, "look I'll prove it, I took pictures,"

Emily excitably struggles to open her phone to pictures and when she has, she places the shot of her foot by the print in front of her mother's face, "look, see I'm telling the truth," Sam takes a long look before Emily prompts her with a "well?" "well it's a foot, a lovely one at that but it's a foot Emily," Emily now confused withdraws the phone and stares at the screen and there to her shock is not a single trace of footprints, she swipes franticly and again no prints, she gives out a small scream of frustration, stomps her feet and as she sprints back upstairs to the landing she hears, "now what would you like for dinner darling?" from her mother, matter-of-factually, Emily reaches the landing and again, stands and stares at bare floorboards whilst asking herself, *where on earth did, they go*, and from deep within the house there comes low deep and slow laughter and she is gripped with fear and at that very moment she knows that there is, indeed, something else other than her father in this house and begins to shake uncontrollably at the thought that whatever it was could mean her harm.

That evening over dinner Emily asks Sam if she could sleep in her room that night. At first Sam feels a slight tinge of resentment as if saying to herself, *for crying out loud Emily, pull yourself together*, but then she stopped herself and looked at her daughter, this young fully grown woman despite her age was still a child and *so what if she was struggling with the death of her father, she had every right to do so and who was she to judge and it didn't matter how Emily comes to terms with this just so long as she does even if that means she sees 'ghosts,* "of course you can sleep with me tonight; we'll see if there's a rubbish movie on to fall asleep to darling."

Both fell fast asleep and indeed to a rubbish movie and they slept sound until morning break and there were no further incidents. Sam was up and out early to see clients and Emily wasn't too far behind, she made breakfast and sat at the Island and ate whilst she watches the news and again, it was a daily ritual of tragic events, it would seem that as the rates of infected went up the more the NHS was being placed under pressure to cope as the flood gates of this pandemic opened and just to make things worse and almost unworkable was the seemingly impossibility of the British government to be able to again supply the simplest of things to them such as surgical gloves, masks and gowns, one of the richest first world countries on the planet and we had well and truly been caught with our pants down and the whole time this sad unfolding story was being punctuated by the daily death toll which was in its hundreds.

It became so unbearable for Emily she had to turn off the tv. *So, what to do* thought Emily, having looked into the fridge and cupboards she realised just how low they were running of supplies and felt surprised that it had been two weeks since her horrible ordeal at the super market, *I know* she thought, *I'll walk into Wicham, they have a small corner store there, I should be able to get some of what we need there*. Wicham was the next village along the lane, but it was still a good one-and-a-half-mile walk and a journey that was indeed undulating such was the topography of this corner of Suffolk, one thing in Emily's favour was the weather which had settled down and was quite spring like again. Emily pulls on a pair of cut down combats and replaced her flip flops for her hiking boots, tied her hoodie around her waist and grabbed some canvas shopping bags from the pantry and she was ready. She wrote a note, kissed Mr Darcy on the head, locked the door which she had now become accustomed to and stepped into the lane. Emily strikes up a comfortable pace and she is swept along by the sheer beauty of this place; the fields were full of lush green wheat and barley and the hedge rows were filled with aromatic cow parsley and wildflowers. Just then to Emily's right comes a flash of brilliant white which didn't startle her because of its movement, it wasn't fast or erratic but smooth and agile as it glided by, and there, no more than feet away from her and about three feet off the ground was the most beautiful, majestic, brilliant white barn owl that now filled her with peace and tranquillity, and there came a slight tinge of curiosity as the owl seemed to be looking directly at her, as if somehow it knew her. Emily spots the owl on a number of further twists and turns of the lane and is struck by the thought that perhaps it is in fact following her and before she knew it, she reaches the brow of the hill that leads down into the village of Wicham and all feeling of calmness quickly slipped away as she was now filled once again with the feeling of dread at the thought that she was to again experience the fear of shopping and coming into contact with people.

On approaching the Wicham corner store Emily pulled on her mask and surgical gloves and gave out a deep anxious exhale of air as she tried to steel herself for what was to come. Ding-a-ling went the bell above the door as Emily opens it just enough to slide through trying desperately not to be noticed, "hello," comes the greeting from behind the counter and there is what Emily presumes is the storekeeper, "hello" says Emily, "how are you my dear," the lady had spoken to her as if she knew her and to Emily's recollection, she had never been in the store before, "I'm fine thank you" says Emily somewhat surprised and for a moment she forgets her manners, "and how are you" "good, good, looking for anything in particular" asks the lady, "um, well just general stuff" as Emily picks up a basket, "ok well let me know if you need any Help," Emily looks around and from that greeting and the fact that the store is empty of people she is able to actually feel somewhat more at ease.

The store was your classic old English corner store with shelves piled high and deep with just about everything from avocados, to boot laces and all in between, and you just knew that if you asked the store owner for the most unlikely of item that after a moment of careful thought she would take you right to where it lay hidden, just waiting for you. With the now thankful feeling of relief Emily takes her time as she scans the goods and is pleasantly surprised to see items, she didn't think they made any more.

After spending more time then she thought she would, Emily finally steps up to the counter with her laden basket, pays and after leaving the store realises that the lady wouldn't have seen her genuine smile because of the mask but, *hey, that was actually a pleasant experience.*

By the time Emily reaches the top of the hill leading out of the village she now knows the return journey was going to be a little slower than the journey in due to the weight of the shopping bags laden with goodies, but she felt pleased and happy as she thought to herself, *I've actually found a way to get supplies without running that gauntlet of dread.* It was an uneventful walk back, not much in the way of sight-seeing as she just wanted to get back and on a couple of occasions she had to put the bags down to take a break but before long she rounded the corner and she was back in her lane. On making her way back in she lumped the bags down with relief and spies Mr Darcy who had obviously not moved a muscle all morning, "Its ok for you, you great big furry lump." After unpacking Emily makes a sandwich and a drink and is heading for the garden to take a nice slow relaxed lunch when she passes the shelving in the living room and she is stopped dead in her tracks, she slowly backs up, turns her head to the right and for a moment stands and stares at the shelf of fossils. That bottle, the heavy one she had stood back up after it supposedly fell over all by itself was now again laying on its side, Emily slowly looks around the room and then comes back to the bottle, "no way, not again," she says to herself, she puts her plate down but instead of picking the bottle back up straight away she bends and looks to see what direction the bottle is pointing, and she follows this across the room to see that its pointing directly to the fireplace, she straightens takes in the information, murmurs, "curious," and on this occasion she lifts the bottle and isn't quite so careful in placing it back onto its exact position as before and continues on with her lunch, all be it in a somewhat reflective mood. That night at dinner Emily asks, "Mum, where did Dad find that bottle in his collection?" "what bottle darling?" "you know, the mottled green one on his shelves in the living room" "oh that thing, no he didn't find that, it was already here" "what!" "yes, it came with the house darling."

Another day and another breakfast accompanied by the latest problems that this pandemic was bringing and of course the latest death toll and this morning it would seem that the government had neglected to foresee an emerging and tragic situation concerning care homes. Emily had enough, enough of the seemingly unnecessary tragedy, it was starting to annoy her, so she switches off the tv and turns on some music. Because Emily was the good student that she was, she had already gone above and beyond the tasks set by her tutor and now genuinely had nothing left to study and she was restless, she began to wander from room to room and at each turn she could see her father captured in a moment as if she were seeing him in a movie scene that kept playing over and over again. Here in the living room she could see him at that last Christmas stood bare foot by the fireplace unwrapping the present Mum had got him, he was in his tartan pyjama bottoms and a long sleeve sweatshirt that was older than her, on its front it had the words, 'The Cure', his eyes lit up and his face broke into a wonderful smile of joy and surprise as he unwrapped the Mont Blanc pen mum had got him.

Emily thought about lounging around in the garden but every time she did, she could see dad at the BBQ or raking excess weed out of the pond for the benefit of the frogs. That was it she could not take this anymore and Emily knew what she was about to do, and she marched off to the under stairs cupboard, there she finds the dyson carpet cleaner and rescues it from the collective clutter, it could be said that over these last couple of months dusting and hoovering had of course been the last thing on the agender and on their minds and Emily could see that there was now a real need to have a good old-fashioned spring clean and she also arms herself with dusters and cloths to boot and sets about her chores with gusto. Some four hours later and there was before her, a fresh and sparkly new home and as she stood exhausted and admired her good deeds and hard work and thought to herself *how pleased is mum going to be with me*. Emily squeezes the dyson back in amongst all the clutter that you would expect to find in anyone's under stair cupboard and is about to close the door when she spot's something that immediately captures her attention and at the very moment she is asking herself, *what is that*? she instantly recognises and knows exactly what 'it' is. There pushed to the back sat a large opaque plastic bag, its neck tightened and tied with a plastic cord and Emily knew that this was the evidence bag that the police officer had placed in the back of their car after her and Sam had gone to identify her father at the morgue. Emily slid down the door and sat staring at this bag for how long she did not know, she fought with herself all this time as to whether she should open this, for what? what reason? what good could come of it? would it only serve to bring back memories and what if it did? would she not be able to cope? Emily uncrossed her legs and jumped up, she teased the bag out and into the hall, the bag wasn't too heavy and she was able to close the cupboard behind her whilst still carrying the bag with one hand. Having taken the bag to the kitchen Emily now found herself looking at the handwritten tag that was attached to the cord and it reads,

D/C HUGHES 7248 SCD4 CLP 14/02/20 12:43pm

FOOD HALL, APPLE MARKET COVENT GARDEN

But it's what comes next that send a short sharp stab directly into her heart,

WILLIAMS OLIVER JAMES DR. DECEASED.

Emily drops the tag, reels back and if it had not been for a stool, she may have found herself on the floor, she sits, and she sobs. After a time, Emily pulls herself together and continues to try and tease the knot in the plastic cord apart with her fingernails, she had contemplated taking a sharp knife to it but she dismissed that thought as she wanted to preserve this package in all its entirety, although she didn't quite know why. Eventually the knot seemed to relent and just untwine seemingly all by itself. Emily prises open the bag and there within sits her father's rucksack. She opens the neck of the bag as wide as she can and lifts the ruck sack out and on doing so she can see a good proportion of the lower part of the ruck sack is covered in blood all be it dried blood, she has no idea if this was her fathers but still it makes Emily sick to her stomach, she takes control of herself once again as she flattens out the plastic evidence bag on the kitchen floor to sit the rucksack on, although the blood seemed dry, she didn't want to take the risk of getting any on the stone flags. Emily unzips the front pocket and finds a number of pens and her father's wallet, there's the expected credit cards, ID for the hospital and a number of receipts but Emily also finds a picture of her mother and a picture of her as a baby, shock of red hair and all, she had no idea the picture even existed. She puts everything back neatly in place and opens the main compartment of the rucksack, there she finds a small leather covered box, the lid of which is spring loaded, and she must force it to open, the interior of the box has a red velvet lining and there nestled in its folds was a ring of silver, its side exquisitely carved and it held a beautiful stone the like of which she had not seen before. Emily snaps the lid shut and puts the box to one side and peers back into the rucksack to find a larger package covered in crepe paper of a wonderful blue colour. She pulls the package out and places it on the work surface of the island, she slides her fingers under the sticky tape and tries very hard not to rip the paper as she prises the two apart, soon she is unfolding the leaves and there before her is a journal, its bound in a rich thick leather and the artwork is a wonderful swirl of differing blues, a depiction of planet earth. Emily hesitates for a moment unsure as to whether she can or wants to touch the journal, for she knows that it is special. She delicately lifts the corner with her fingertips and is greeted with the sound of creaking and groaning from the spine and the smell of leather and paper envelops her and there inside the cover is writing, writing she knows all too well.

To my dearest darling Emily

I wish you all the happiness in the world

On this incredibly special day, your 18th birthday

and although Circumstance means I cannot be with you in person

I want you to know I shall always be with you in

Spirit, you're forever loving Father Oliver xxx

P.s here's somewhere to keep all your special thoughts.

Emily was struck by an overwhelming feeling that someone was standing behind her and she freezes with fearful anticipation as to whether this whatever it was enveloping her would be vengeful and spiteful but her fears were unfounded as a feeling of peaceful tranquillity began to wrap itself around her and she closed her eyes and exhaled deeply. Whether this was the spirit of her father or not she knew it meant her no harm. Sam came home that evening and it struck Emily that she had not had a particularly good day and didn't say very much to Emily until she was pouring her second glass of wine, she most certainly didn't make an effort to mention anything about the sterling job Emily had made of the cleaning, perhaps she hadn't noticed. Emily pours herself a glass which seemed to aggravate her mother further, "hey should you be drinking that what with the drugs and all?" "thanks for reminding me, but one can't hurt," said Emily, "how was your day" asked Sam, "it was ok, didn't get up to much, dare I inquire as to yours" "absolutely bloody awful, I mean how am I supposed to bloody work like this, they have absolutely no idea the kind of pressure that they are placing me under, with little to no direction coming out of them" "who?" ask Emily, "the bloody government, concerning the welfare of the racing industry," there came a pause as Sam takes another gulp of wine, "well this might cheer you up" says Emily as she produces the ring box from her pocket, places it on the work surface and slides it towards Sam, who just stares at the box, "it's a…" "I know what it is Emily" "but Dad bought it for you Mum" "I know where it came from EMILY!" "but it's a beautiful ring Mum" "THEN YOU HAVE IT," snaps Sam as she springs to attention and goes to walk out, turns picks up the bottle and says, "I would appreciate, Emily if you would desist in snooping around in matters that do not concern you" and she stomps out.

Emily sat deflated, disappointed, her mum up until just recently had dealt with all of this pretty well, or so she thought but of late she had witnessed her mum becoming more frustrated and angry at the mere simplest of things and of course she had taken to drinking more, if this was her way of dealing with this then so be it, she can but only *be there when it all comes crashing down,* she thought, but for now best to let things just settle. Emily drains the last of the wine from her glass and stares at the ring box, she grabs it flips open the lid, takes out the ring and places it on her ring finger of her right hand, sits and admires it for a while, a small smile upon her lips, she then slides from her stool and heads toward her bedroom, she closes the curtains falls onto her bed and she cracks opens the journal, the smell of fresh paper wafts over her and she turns to the first page, picks up her favourite pen, stops to think for a moment for that spark of inspiration and she begins to write.

Do I Belong

By Emily Williams

Tell me, where do I belong,
Amidst this life, this energy, this wrong,
What lies beneath this world of hate?
To embrace it wide or feel my fate,
Bind me with this distant spell,
Entwine me with this ancient cord,
My soul dance on this night fell,
Spirals of flames that eat the horde,
Mindless murmurs and flickers of light,
Stretching sanity bathed in plight,
Let tonight be strong,
Let tonight be bold,
As we are born free,
Sing to awaken the old.

Emily came to with a start, she had fallen asleep on top of her bed, her face stuck to the covers her eyesight blurred, she couldn't focus as her head was thumping, she knew it was morning or what was left of it as she could hear birds singing outside her window and there was light streaming in from the window which was now making her wince as she found it hard to just open her eyes, let alone focus. *why am I feeling so rough,* thought Emily? *for crying out loud Emily, it was only one glass of wine, you light weight,* but in her defence, she was on a cocktail of sedatives and it was the first time she had any alcohol for as long as she could remember, but no matter how she tried to dress this up she felt rough and to make things worse she was shivering, she didn't know whether it was because she had slept on top of the bed in nothing but t-shirt and shorts, the alcohol or the rather changeable weather that would seem to fluctuate day by day for this morning it had decided to be overcast and noticeably chilly.

Emily peeled herself from her bed and there, still open in front of her was the journal her father had bought her and to her disappointment and anger she had torn the first page out; she knew she had written something last night, but what? she couldn't at this moment quite remember, but had it really been that bad to warrant tearing it from her journal, her present from dad, how stupid of her, she now began to scour the floor around her bed, nothing, what on earth would she have done with that, she looked in her wastepaper basket by her desk, again nothing, there then comes a roll of thunder from beyond her window and she feels a cold shiver running over her body and she suddenly realises that she needs tea to help her think straight.

Emily puts her hoodie on and zips it, she pulls the hood up and pushed her hands into the sleeves, in an attempt to gain some warmth. Walking downstairs had apparently become something that she could no longer do properly as an adult as her legs and back felt stiff and awkward and she had to unsheathe her hands to steady herself by grabbing the railing. The stone floor in the kitchen felt cold beneath her bare feet but also somewhat soothing as she reached for the kettle to switch it on and she then becomes aware of Mr Darcy scratching at the kitchen door to be let out, *unusual* she thought, *he must be desperate*, no sooner as she had cracked opened the door did Mr Darcy force and squeeze his way out to flee at pace to a snap of lightning breaking the air over head, "steady Mr D." Emily returned to the kettle and this time clunks it into life and again slipped her hands into her sleeves and gave a large yawn, her eyes now sprang open wide as she is jolted into a coherent state, she wasn't ready for as there came from the front of the house the same three low deep thuds she had heard before when she thought that her father had embraced her, but there was something else, something that shook and frightened her to her core, SMOKE, she could smell smoke. Emily pads through the house at speed but consciously peering around each corner first before entering the room, she knew where she was going, to the front room, the oldest part of the house, the old court room and where she had first encountered the bangs.

Before she got to the doorway, she could see her entrance was blocked, her sight of the interior marred by thick dense smoke and against all common sense she enters, the sensible thing to have done was to leave and call the fire service, but Emily was now acting out of impulse, *their wonderful family home was on fire*, Emily burst in, smoke swirling and spiralling around her and everything slowed and became muffled and darkened, she could hear voices but not what they were saying, out of the smog she could make out the heads of people, seated, their faceless heads all in a row, again a voice to her right, but she did not turn to look for appearing before her through the smoke came a box like structure and stood within it is a person who she now begins to focus upon, and as this structure comes towards her the features of this person now become clearer. Emily begins to get the feeling that she was in court and the person before her was in the dock, but it was the expression upon this person's face that shook Emily.

There before her was a young girl, clad in a grey long sleeved dress with a pinafore tied about her, a bonnet upon her head with streams of long golden hair falling about her shoulders and arms, but it was her eyes, the eyes within this youthful pretty face were wide, none blinking, transfixed on her, this child was terrified for her very life and as Emily went to speak, to say something, to try and make contact there came a voice to her right, now crystal clear and shouted, "WITCH", and with this the smoke that had obscured the room before dissipated as if a strong wind had just blown through and with it the vision of this young girl, her sorrowful eyes the last to disappear into the mist. Emily was left standing in the middle of their front room, no smoke, no smell, no noise, just calm, just their old front room and Emily was overcome with a feeling of weakness as if all energy had been drained from her very veins she felt dizzy and sick and knew this had nothing to do with alcohol nor drugs and they had nothing to do with what she had just witnessed either. Regardless as to whether her mother believed her or not Emily now knew for herself that there was indeed a spirit or spirits within the house one of which she knew was this girl in the dock, who was she? why was she on trial? had she been the one who had made the wet footprints? and why had the voice cried "witch?"

All Emily knew for now was she had to find out, the way this girl had looked at her told her that she was in trouble and needed her help, quite how she was going to do that? right now she knew not how; Emily jumps out of her skin from the noise of the kettle in the kitchen switching itself off and she shakes her head at being caught like that, her nerves were in tatters.

Emily turns to her laptop and does all the usual searches such as Wikipedia and after a frustrating couple of hours comes to the curious conclusion that there has been little to no information written about, her village in all its years. She finds a reference and records office in Bury St Edmunds but again information is limited, and she soon comes to a dead end when the site informs her that to be able to go any further with her inquiries, she would have to attend the office in person with photo ID and proof of address which in the current climate was impossible do to the fact that everything was closed because of covid 19. *Who could I talk too, who would know?* Just then a face comes to mind and Emily says out loud, "Mr Aston."

Emily had known Mr Benjamin Aston for all her years, he had supposedly lived in the village for all of his, a teacher for all his career, he had taught in local schools, but Emily had not the pleasure of him as a tutor but she had gone to him when she was in high school to ask for advice concerning a history project and he was so kind in helping her that she'd got top marks for what she submitted, so if there were ever a person that would know of the history of this tiny village then it will be he, Mr Aston, the self-proclaimed local historian. Emily strolled through the village and as she came to Mr Aston's cottage, she was filled with a tinge of gilt as she hadn't spoken to him since the project, and since then Mr Aston had become a widower.

As she placed a hand onto the gate of the white picket fence the door of the cottage came open and there stood Mr Aston. "Well hello my dear, what a pleasant surprise" "hello Mr Aston, it's Emily Williams, I don't know if you remember me" "well of course I do Emily, please come in."

Emily felt relief as she walked through the gate and beamed a big smile but soon had to halt in her tracks as she remembered the two-metre rule and the smile was replaced with a frown.

On seeing this Mr Aston enquired, "Emily, I gather you have been isolating, haven't you?" "yes, I have Mr Aston" "well in that case I think you and I can safely forgo this awful two metre distancing thing, don't you," and the smile comes back to Emily's face, "would you care for a cup of tea Emily," Emily still smiling nods with approval, "and I think we can also forgo this Mr Aston thing too, don't you, please call me Ben" "Ok Ben it is," says Emily. Ben shows Emily through his cottage which is small but neat and tidy and out into the back garden which is just as well-kept and offers Emily a seat at the garden table, parasol and all. "how do you take your tea?" "white no sugar please," as Ben goes to turn, he pauses and says "I was deeply sorry to hear of your father's death Emily, although I had only met him on a couple of occasions, he did strike me as a kindly man" "thank you Ben," he gives a small smile, "now let me see to that tea."

Ben soon returns with a tray, atop is a teapot, two cups with saucers, a small milk jug and a plate with two digestive biscuits, exactly how one would expect English afternoon tea to be served, Emily stands and makes the gesture for Mr Aston to be seated as she takes charge of serving the tea to the obvious delight of Ben. Emily first pours Ben's then hers and put just a small dash of milk in each and places Ben's tea in front of him, there is a small pause as there comes the clinks of spoons stirring tea. "Now, as much as I'm utterly thrilled to see you my dear, I do gather that there is a reason for your visit is there not?" Emily replaces her cup to saucer having just taken a sip, "yes, Mr, sorry Ben, I was wondering whether you would know very much of my home, Willow Cottage," "ahhh yes, Willow Cottage." Ben and Emily talk long into the afternoon over more tea and biscuits and not all about her home and the history of the village, they had also reminisced about Ben's wife who had died some years earlier and there had also been talk of happier times for them both and as Emily closes the front gate and waves Ben good bye she thinks to herself, *I actually meant what I just said to Ben, I shall come back to visit for tea, and regularly.*

Emily strolls back along the lane and thinks to herself, *ok, so let me see if I've got this right, some three hundred or so years ago some French count by the name of Bourbonne builds a manor house on our lane and whilst he's at it he builds a brewery, an abattoir and a courthouse, which just happens to be our willow Cottage. The count has a son who has an affair with one of their servants, Annie Wright, gets her pregnant and the count has her murdered by the then witch finder general, a Mathew Hopkins and she apparently is drowned in our pond,* Emily comes to a sudden stop in the lane prompted by a realisation, "oh my word", says Emily out loud, "that was the girl I saw in the dock, that was Annie wright," Emily moves on, *ok, so count and son duel, son dies and sometime later count die's when manor house burns down,* then Ben had mentioned that some of the salvage materials from the manor house had gone to build Owlsden Hall and subsequently then found its way to helping in the building of our extensions at Willow Cottage, he had said that I might want to seek out the local builder Chris Carter, who had done those extensions for the then owner back in the nineties, quite why she didn't know? but hey all and any information to try and help solve this.

The following morning Emily had a silent breakfast, she simply didn't want to turn the tv on, it had become to depressive concerning the virus and somewhat frustrating as to the lack of information and direction from the government, moreover, there seemed to be an unease in certain sections of the population not just in the UK but also in the USA that had led to some sporadic rioting and looting. Emily pads bare foot through to the front room that was now bathed in early morning sun light, cereal bowl still in hand and stands for a while and watches and listens and all is still and quiet, "I know now who you are Annie, I know you are Annie Wright, and I know they accused you of being a witch," Emily waited but nothing came from the room, she gave a small shrug and resumed eating her cereal and was about to return to the kitchen when she was stopped by what she thought was a growl or groan coming from their living room but as she reached this space there was nothing, no sounds, no smell, no presence to be felt. On sliding back onto the stool in the kitchen, laptop open in front of her she noticed in the corner of the screen the time and there below the date and she became motionless for a brief second, 14/06/2020, had it really been four months since her father's death, what with the pandemic and having to isolate she had lost all sense of time but what had upset her the most is that she hadn't even been to visit his grave since the day of the funeral. Emily Takes a pair of scissors into the garden and gathers some peonies and some roses that had been a particular favourite of Oliver's and places these in the kitchen sink with some water whilst she showers and puts on an off the shoulder long light summer dress and of course her flip flops, she ties up her hair and with a quick look out of the window decides to take with her a short cardigan, just in case. She gathers up the flowers, says goodbye to Mr D, locks the door and stroll's up the lane towards the church.

Emily was quite struck with just how much everything had grown in the short few months since she and Sam had laid Oliver to rest, it must be this combination of warm weather and storms she thought, she pushed open the church gate and walked directly to Oliver's grave, there she laid the flowers down, "hello Dad." Emily sat at the foot of Oliver's grave, the grass warm and dry and she spoke of all the things since that had happened, the pandemic, college closing, being isolated, but despite this 'Mum' had seemed to be busier than ever and in fact there was talk of late that some of the easing of lock down restriction may be the lifting on the ban of horse racing, so she could become even busier, said Emily, she talked and talked and Oliver listened, she felt, he was there, like he said, *if not in person, in spirit, and would always be.*

Over those two or so hours that Emily kept Oliver company she had felt not just the presence of her father but something else, that of being watched, it wasn't oppressive nor threatening and in fact, gave a sense of being guarded, perhaps this was Oliver too, 'a fathers protection', in the midst of a comfortable pause Emily glances skyward and to the line of oaks that ringed the graveyard and up on high she spies a barn owl, its glare fixed directly upon her. It wasn't unusual to see owls here abouts even in broad daylight, after all the place was synonymous with them but it was the fact that this owl would not break from its stare upon her, but again It didn't unnerve her it was in fact quite reassuring. Emily hoped that she hadn't babbled too much and she was pleased that she hadn't wept either even when she had gotten up, brushed herself down, kissed her fingertips bent and placed her fingers on the top of Oliver's gravestone, "bye Dad, love you, see you soon," as she turned to walk away, she looked up at the owl, "bye owl, watch over him for me, will you," and for the first time the owl gave a little shuffle in response.

Emily re-joined the graveyard path and walked back slowly toward the gate; she was glad she had spoken to her father, she was at peace, when just then she glances sideways at an incredibly old gravestone and from it a name that jolts her from her tranquil state, the name of 'Bourbonne.' Emily stepped from the path and to the head stone, she kneels and rubs away the moss that covers the inscription and reads.

HERE LIETH THE SOUL OF LOUIS

DEARLY BELOVED SON OF KATHRINE

AND THE COUNT BOURBONNE
revenged
THOU SHALT BE ~~MISSED~~ IN THIS LIFE

AND NEXT

BORN MARCH 4TH, 1629 DIED AUGUST 6TH, 1647

Emily finished reading the epitaph but had to go back to the word 'missed' for it had a line clearly scratched through it and above this the word 'revenged' carved which struck Emily as quite curious as this was no modern defacing or graffiti this altering of the wording had clearly been done an exceedingly long time ago, but there was something else, the date of Louis's death, 1647, if he had died in a duel with his father on that day then it figures that was also the day that Annie Wright was put to death in her pond, August 6th, 1647.

Emily had now taken to listening to the radio as opposed to switching on the tv as there was nothing but news and bad news at that, however, between the tunes there inevitably came bulletins and of course they were all about the pandemic and how it was affecting the world and of course, it was harrowing, sorrowful and disturbing and there did come yet another feeling that Emily was finding difficult to control, that of anger. Over the previous few days there had been a relaxing of the 'lock down/ quarantine' rules and it would seem that the great British public had taken that as the green light to party in the streets and or go to the beach in their tens of thousands, it was as if at that given moment the virus had ceased to exist and despite all the warnings about 'infection rates' and 'social distancing', and so it was on that day, mid-June, our coastal regions and beauty spots were swamped and overwhelmed by hordes of stupid and really rather selfless people. Rage flowed through Emily as she paced the kitchen and gave a really, rather plausible argument concerning this utterly silly situation to a seemingly unconcerned and somewhat comatose Mr D. Emily stamps her foot in frustration as the anger rises within her and just then as quickly as it came, this swelling of hatred is quelled by the sound of her father, and his voice saying to her troubled mind in his own words, *to put down all your thoughts and feelings as they affected you darling*, she grabs for her journal opens it and after a slight twinge of regret and subsequent guilt of having seemingly ripped out the front page and discarding it, she knows not where, she begins to write furiously.

Deep Medication

By Emily Williams

The light slips into the dark room

Touching the surface, searching the bloody womb

Like a worm threading through the dark

Seeking out places that are dear to your heart

Is it my mind overthinking or more?

Or is it reality scratching outside my door

I hold my breath not daring to live

You coming for me? You making me give

It claws out my soul, every step feels my last

You prise out my mind the void is so vast

Let me sleep, let me rest

My eyes close tight I do not feel blessed.

Having spent her pent-up aggression across the page, Emily slumps back in her seat with an overwhelming feeling of fatigue and her mind wanders back to the house and recent events. She now begins to feel that her initial thought that it was her father's presence she was experiencing in the house was wrong, and in fact it was Annie that had put her arms around her on several occasions, and she recalled that one time in particular when she had gone to enter the front room and she had felt arms about her, was this Annie? holding her back, had she not wanted her to go in, after all it was here that she had heard with her own ears a man's voice shouting the word 'WITCH,' and then there was the uncomfortable feeling of being watched all the time, and she remembered the wet footprints that had mysteriously disappeared on the landing, and that evil laughter coming from within the house, and why had she just felt so angry and violent just now, and on those notes, Emily had now come to the conclusion that there truly was something else here, another spirit and one that had nothing but evil intent. Emily rests her head against the back of the chair and closes her eyes, she was that tired she could easily go to sleep right there and then, suddenly there came a realisation to her, the hoodie she was in, was the same hoodie she'd had on when she walked into the front room / courthouse and it stank of smoke and as she lifts the front of it up to her nose and sniffs, she says out loud, "phew!" and on doing so she catches a whiff of herself and realises that she too, doesn't smell so great either, *I think I'm in need of a wash, I know I'll have a nice long relaxing soak*, and she lifts herself and pads upstairs.

Emily opens the hot tap full and water cascades into a beautiful deep white porcelain free standing tub with large golden lions feet at each corner that keeps it some six inches off the tiled floor. Emily leans over the bath and pops open the small diamond leaded window to allow the now billowing steam to escape. She scans the glass shelving over the bath and spots a small bottle of lavender oil, unscrews the cap, takes a sniff and thinks, *yes, that will help to relax me*, and gently pours a couple of drops into the now rapidly filling bath, she then picks up a large plastic bottle and it's not the initial wording of 'vanilla and orchid' that makes her smile but the following words of 'Double the Bubble Bath' and she put a good dollop or three in and watches as it all becomes frothy. Having retrieved her dressing gown and flip flops from her bedroom she returns and strips, places her smelly clothes in the wash basket and having stepped into the bath gingerly now sets about dipping her body oh so gently into the hot water inch by inch, 'hot, hot, hot', she hisses. Once Emily has managed to submerge herself fully, she closes her eyes and rests her head on the back of the bath and exhales long and slow. *This was such a good idea* she thinks, as she can feel all the stress just seeping out from her body. Emily had lost all track of time and in fact she couldn't work out whether she had fallen asleep or not, but she was jerked back into this world with a shock, but what had shaken her was not of this world, all laws of logic had simply been torn apart, how could this be, for she was in a bath six inches off the floor, and yet from beneath the water something had violently grab her right ankle, its grip and force so intense she believed that tibia and fibula were about to be simultaneously crushed, its claws felt like red hot pokers now piercing her skin, but no matter how much Emily kicked she was not going to break its hold. Emily sits bolt upright and goes to give out a huge scream but before a single sound can come from her lips, she is whipped beneath the water at a speed that is totally unnatural, the water settles, the bubbles slowly close in and cover the surface once more and there comes a silence.

Emily knows she is under water as she can feel the pressure of it around her body and she instinctively holds her breath but now she must force herself to open her eyes. Whatever it is that she is in? it felt infinite, despite the fact she is surrounded by a darkness, there felt a deepness beneath her. She glances up at what looks like the underside of a vast ice sheet fading into the dark distance in every direction and there above her some thirty feet away is a small hole, a shaft of brilliant light coming down through it towards her and she knows that's where she had come from, and that's where she must now get back to. She kicks with all her might and surges upwards grabbing hold of fistfuls of water and dragging them down, thankfully whatever had her leg was now no longer there or was it? just below her? roaring back up from the depths to attack her once again and she could not but help let out a scream muffled by bubbles escaping her lungs. She gave thanks for all those lengths she had put in at the college pool, and soon the hole was within reach and thankfully so as she could feel herself running out of air, she burst through the hole and has to inhale deeply before she can scream and her hands grab hold of each side of the bath and it takes all her might to haul herself up and out, all the time fearing that whatever *it* was, *it* would grab her again at any moment to once more drag her beneath, and she wastes no time in throwing herself over the side of the bath and makes no attempt in stopping her wet body slapping the cold tiles as she falls.

Emily lays onto her back coughing and spluttering, trying to suck air and life back into her shivering body, despite how frightened and confused she is she is unable to pick herself up for what seems like minutes, when she is, she rolls and vomits water on the floor, this seems to bring life back to her limbs and she pulls herself up by the bath, grabs her dressing gown and flip flops and runs from the room and back down the stairs and out into the garden, right now she does not want to even be within the house, within those confines, right now she feels the real need for an open sky above her. Emily try's hard to make sense of what just happened to her, but she cannot, it goes beyond all realms of logic. Shaking through fear and cold, its only now that Emily realises that she is standing in her back garden completely naked, dressing gown in one hand flip flops in the other. She was not concerned with being seen, the lane is seldom used and beside the line of protective willows means that the garden is quite secluded, but as of this moment Emily did not care for her modesty, her mind was spinning out of control, if she had any doubt before of the presence of an evil spirit, this was most certainly now dashed, for she now knew that there were indeed spirits and one was most definitely evil, for it had just tried to kill her, of that she was now most definitely certain.

Emily now pulls on her dressing gown and slips on her flip flops and she takes a few awkward steps towards the pond as though she was recovering from a long run, her limbs suffering with lactic acid build up. She pauses in front of the smaller of the two oaks beside the pond, pulls her dressing gown lapels up tight around her neck for some feel of comfort and security and stares, wide eyed off down the garden at nothing in particular, her mind still racing.

From behind Emily the gnarled and twisted bark of the ancient oak begins to oh so slowly move and morph and from within emerges the grotesque and deformed face of a monster, the face of Count Bourbonne, his red eyes of fire now burning into the back of Emily's head. Emily stood still, hands still cradling her face, she was now staring at the ground just feet away from her still not able to make sense of what had just happened to her when deep within her mind a vision began to form, an image that was slowly being pieced together with information received from her peripheral vision and there to her right just at the back of the garden shed there stood a figure, that of a person or creature bent seemingly almost in two, it was clad in a long black cape and out from under a large hood that obscured its face came the rat tail wisps of long silver white hair and as this picture came together within Emily's mind, she jumped so violently that she gave out a small scream. Emily steeled herself and turned to walk toward this thing, its black robes now being blown about by a sudden gust of wind. As Emily moved away from the small oak tree, a knobbly talon like hand of the Count just barely missed digging its claws into Emily's shoulder and for the second time that day the Count missed his opportunity of devouring his prey. Emily totally oblivious to how close she had come to falling into the clutches of Count now curiously tip toed one foot in front of the other toward the creature crouched by the shed and as she came close her whole demeanour suddenly shifted from one of defence and possible flight to one of standing bolt upright, leaning forward and staring intently at what had made her jump out of her skin.

Emily now moved forward and grabbed hold of the black torn tatters of the BBQ cover, those rat-tailed wisps of silver white hair were nothing more than an old white tea towel that had inadvertently been left hanging over one of the BBQ handles from the summer before.

Emily stumbles backwards with a strange mix of emotions, that of utter relief that she hadn't just encountered an actual real-life witch, and that of feeling completely and utterly stupid. Emily with a huff turns on her heels and stomps back toward the house and stuffing her hands into the pockets of her dressing gown to find a small cylindrical pill bottle and as she levels with the pond she pulls the bottle out and looking at it she rattles the pills inside; she pops the cap and saying to herself out loud, "I obviously, for body and mind, can no longer afford to take this crap," and she turns the bottle upside down and tips its contents into the pond. Emily reluctantly re-enters the house and immediately opens all the doors and although she knows that what she had just seen or what she thought she has seen was just a figment of her overactive imagination, drug induced or not, but what had happened to her in the bath was all too real and the deep painful claw marks that burned into her ankle bore this out. Emily sits in a window seat looking out over the driveway with Mr Darcy on her lap for comfort and perhaps a little security. Soon Sam comes rolling into the drive, in the time that Emily had been waiting she had gone over and over as to what she should say to her mother about what had happened to her earlier that day, would she understand? would she even believe her? Emily thought it highly unlikely and so after going through all the scenarios Emily thought it best not to say too much. Sam eventually comes in with all the stories of the day and as horse racing had in fact been given the all clear to resume there had come a ramping up of activity around the studs of Newmarket and thus Sam's talents would now be in much greater demand, which of course would mean she would be away much more including weekends, which gives Emily a sense of mixed emotions, for one she didn't like the idea of being on her own in the house but then she was glad that the more her mother was away the less likely it would be that Sam would have to suffer what she had experienced that day.

Emily had prepared some cold pasta and salad and sat pretty much in silence as her mum spoke excitedly, Emily could see that despite all the false moans groans and complaints her mum was happy and content in her work, and at home, it had been a blessing in disguise her being able to return to work, it had obviously helped her to begin to get over the loss of Oliver. It wasn't until Emily had finished the washing up and was drying her hands that she interrupted her mother, Sam took this pause as a good opportunity to refill her wine glass, "ok mum listen, I have spoken to you before about some of the feelings that I have been experiencing in the house of late" "oh no Emily not this again, what is it this time? chains a rattling?" Emily chose to ignore her mother's attempt at humour and continued, "look, Mum I already know what your thoughts and feelings are concerning this, and I don't need to be reminded nor lectured, I know what I have experienced and am continuing to experience, and this is not an attempt at some form of therapy, i.e. *let's share it with the group shall we Emily*, NO, this is for your benefit Mum, do not under any circumstance be alone in the house, do you understand," her mother now taking it seriously, "but Emily" "never alone, do you hear" "yes…, yes darling, but what's happen for you to be like this" "you don't need to know and trust me it's best you didn't," "I'm off to bed I'll see you in the morning," Sam was left with the feeling that in no uncertain terms she had just been told 'what's what' by her daughter and from Emily's stance she wasn't, for now about to argue with that, she simply re-charged her glass and switched on the tv. Emily reached the top of the stairs and was feeling rather pleased with herself, she had changed, become stronger in herself she thought and as she entered the bathroom room to clean her teeth, all thought of this newfound confidence was dashed as she pulled the light on and there was the bath still full, what with all that had happened she had not returned there all day and had forgotten all about the water, she now pulls the plug and watches the water spiral away with a gurgle and as it does Emily slowly crouches and looks under the bath and yes just as she had thought, there was nothing, just a six-inch gap between the bath and the tiles, Emily cleans her teeth one eye looking over her shoulder via the mirror and before she turns in Emily once again turns to her journal for some comfort and guidance and she writes.

The Awakening
By Emily Williams

What are these feelings thou has placed in my hands?

The eternal place of home that lay beneath these lands

Come gather my thoughts for I am be told

The spirit that entwines will never grow old

Feel the call drifting into the night

Begging my soul to be guided to the light

I feel that you are with me

Live with me in death for all eternity.

The phone rings, "hi Sam it's me" "hi Joe, how's things" "same old, same old, but hey its Wednesday, fancy a drink" "do you think we should, what about isolating" "well you've worn a mask everywhere you've been, and I've been nowhere except stuck in here with this three-way comedy act and I don't mind telling you Sam, I'm just about going stir crazy here, and besides have you seen all those idiots flocking to the beach? go on Sam, we'll social distance around your island" "ok, when are you coming" "I'll wait till dark and I'll walk, you know what some people are like around here" "ok, do you want to eat with us?" "no, I just need a drink, I've got to rustle something up for this lot anyway, so I'll grab a bite with them and be over, but thanks anyway" "ok, see you soon, bye, bye, bye."

Joe slips in through the kitchen door of Willow cottage like a thief in the night, with her bag of swag which she swings onto the island and Sam peers in to find two bottles of red wine, "what's the prosecco for" "pre drinks, drink", says Joe and Sam puts one hand to her forehead, "you are totally incorrigible Joe, I'm supposed to be working tomorrow" "go in late, come on Sam? this whole corona thing is starting to get just a little too much, we deserve this," Sam shakes her head and says, "you'll be the death of me Joe" "you know it makes sense," says Joe as she sets about popping the fizz with a broad grin and Sam pulls down a couple of glasses. Joe was right this had long been overdue and as the two settled in they clinked glasses and as they did it seemed just for a moment thing had just gone back to normal.

One bottle in and Joe cracks open one of the bottles of red whilst Sam organises some crackers and a selection of nice cheese, "how's Emily?" asked Joe, "don't ask," says Sam with a deep sigh, "oh, is she having problems?" "no, not at seeing ghosts, she isn't," "what!" "yeah, she thinks she can feel the presence of her father and then there was this thing about footprints appearing in the house" "and was there?" "no Joe, of course there wasn't any, "and just recently she took it upon herself to tell *me* that *I* was not to be, under any circumstance, alone in *my* own home, at any time, can you believe that?" "*no*, is she still on her meds?" "yes and I'm thinking of asking Dr Hendricks to up the dose" "so you think it's the drugs" "well yes of course, I mean we all have 'ghosts,' you know the odd bang and thump, doors opening that sort of thing, even your place can feel a bit weird at times Joe" "no that's just the kids and hubby Sam", and they laugh, "do you remember Sam that time shortly after you and Oliver had moved in and one night the whole cottage moved by itself and the following day at the shop you enquired about the 'earthquake''', and again, the two rolled about with laughter.

Emily stirs and begins to come to and realises from the heavy hungover feeling that she had obviously slept sound once again, so sound that she hadn't heard her mum leave that morning. She was dry, dehydrated and was in desperate need of a cup of tea. She puts on her hoodie and pulls the hood up, slides on flip flops and walks out onto the landing, she body- swerves the bathroom door and thinks, *teeth can be cleaned later, besides, I don't need a fight this morning.* As Emily reaches the kitchen, she realises with surprise that her mum is still here, "oh, I thought you had gone already" "no, I've pushed back my appointments for this morning," Emily goes to the kettle, fills it and pop's it on and there beside the sink are the empty bottles from the night before, "have a party, did we?" "yes, something like that, Joe came over" "and must have passed out by the look of it," Emily says on turning, "EMILY, what on earth have you done to your hair?" Emily panics and grabs her head, "what do you mean mum?" "take a look in the mirror darling," Emily rushes through to the living room and to the large mirror above the fireplace, she looks at her reflection and there just peeping out from under her hood is a tuft of brilliant white hair, Emily yanks the hood off, and the tuft turns into one long single ringlet of what was vibrant red and is now a snowy white streak smack bang in the middle of her hair line.

Emily, utterly speechless walks slowly back to the kitchen holding the white ringlet before her, "well, that's not like you Emily, but I have to say, I do quite like it, right I'm off, I've fed Mr D, I'll pick us up something for dinner," and with a flurry of activity Sam grabs her bag, keys and just like that she's out the door and gone.

Emily is stood, still stunned holding out this light lock before her shocked eyes and she says to herself, *I've now taken to dying my own hair in the middle of the night, have I? ok, first the journal and now this*, she returns to the mirror and stares at herself, first one way then the next, and she had to agree with mum it did indeed look quite stylish on her.

Emily takes a call from her tutor at college and organises some new assignments and makes no mention of what she has experienced and finds it difficult to lie when her tutor asked if everything was ok. With little more than a day's course work to do Emily decides to leave it for a rainy day but that now leaves a dilemma in that she doesn't want to be around the house much on her own, so she decides to get herself out and go for a good long walk, she checks the weather app and although it says it's to stay fine, she still takes a thin waterproof and a small bottle of water, she thinks about taking her journal, finding a spot to do some writing but decides against it, *what if it does rain, she thinks.* She dons a pair of walking boots, leaves a window open for Mr D and locks the door and strides into the lane and immediately slows her pace as she instantly feels the shroud of heavy pressure fall away although she is only yards from the cottage. She has no idea of her course and does not care; for she feels safe and breathes deeply of the summer air and was content to waft along and allow the warm scented breeze to carry her wherever it pleased. Emily stuck to the fields via public footpaths, she had no wanting to meet anyone and if this pandemic had shown her anything it was how little she needed company, however, as it happens she did indeed have a friend, all be it that of a young girl, who happened to be a ghost and a not so wanted demonic entity that in fact wanted *her* dead, "you couldn't write this," and she feigns a small smile at the thought. Emily soon found herself at a fields edge and there before her was the village of Wickham.

I know, she thought, *I'll go to that shop and pick up a few bits,* Emily see's the same lady behind the counter, *she has to be the owner.* Emily thinks *as she is always here,* and there came the same reassuring smile as Emily comes through the door that made her not only feel welcome but safe, and Emily takes her time as she peruses the shelves and wonders how on earth does this lady sell half of this stuff as most of it seems so random and obscure and the fact that some items have dust on them bares out the length of time they had spent waiting for that one person to walk in and say, "just what I've been looking for." Emily spends too long in the store and thus spends too much money, and by the time she leaves she has two bags full of stuff she's not quite sure she needs, *hey ho* she thinks as the bell on the door dings her departure.

One hundred yards up the road and Emily is already regretting some of the purchases she had made as her fingers, forearms and shoulders are beginning to ache and it's not just her that she is wondering whether will make it home or not, she is beginning to have doubts about the flimsy plastic bags that she had to buy as well. Emily places the two bags down gentle and straightens to catch a moment of rest and she finds herself looking at a line of ex local authority properties to her left and although she was staring in their direction, she wasn't much caring until the end terrace captured her attention, for it would seem this property more so than the others had been extended in every possible way one could imagine, she was about to use the term '*improved*' but she stopped herself just short of doing so. There parked in the drive was a white transit van and written down the side in capitals was CHRIS CARTER BUILDER and under was his mobile number and Emily's thoughts go back to the meeting she had with Benjamin, "seek out the builder who did the work on Willow cottage" he had said. Emily picks up her shopping, walks to the gate places it down again before going through the gate and up the garden path, she rings the doorbell and steps back a respectful six feet, she was fairly sure he'd be there, after all it was Friday and after four pm.

There came footsteps and the door was wrenched open with a shudder. "Hi, are you Chris Carter?" "that's me, what can I do for you?" Chris is in his early to mid-fifties and wiry, you can tell he does a physical job and tanned, very tanned, the look and texter of old cracked leather, "Hi I'm Emily Williams," Chris looks at her quizzically, "you worked on my mum and dads house, willow Cottage, Owlsden," "oh yeah... what's wrong with it?" "nothing" "good, how's your mum and dad," he's now smiling again, "mum's ok, dads dead," he now frowns, and has a problem with taking in and processing the last piece of information, "I was wondering if you can help me please?" asks Emily, "sure but I have to warn you I'm completely booked out for the rest of this year, what is it you need doing?" "it's actually, some information I'm after," "oh yeah, about what" "you did the extensions on our house back in the mid-nineties, didn't you?" Chris's character changes to that of slightly defensive, "and what if I did?" "nothing's wrong, I'd just like to know what it was that you found Mr Carter," Chris's whole demeanour now changes again to one of slightly aggressive, Emily hadn't known exactly what if anything was found, she was playing a bluff off the back of Benjamin's suggestion, Chris closes the door behind him as if to stop anyone in the house from hearing the conversation, and on turning back to Emily she hears him say under his breath, "I knew this would come back to bite me in the arse one day," he now faces Emily, she says nothing, she knew that if the bluff were to work, she would have to stand her ground and not say another word, Chris moves towards her but only by a step as he sees that she's not budging. "Ok, right listen in, I'm not about to get mugged off or take any shit because of that arsehole Broomfield and if you or anyone has a problem with that then I suggest you take it up with him, do I make myself clear?" "Yes, crystal, Mr Carter" says Emily, surprising herself with how calm she appears outwardly, there's a pause before Chris says, "remains," "what human," says Emily, "well, yeh darling, what do *you* think, the family dog," "so, you dug up the remains of a human," "allegedly" says Chris with a hint of coy, "so was that a problem?" "to Broomfield it was, you're supposed to inform the police about that sort of thing" "and Bromfield didn't want to?" "nah, it would have delayed the build for six weeks or more and as I had other jobs lined up, I wouldn't have been able to come back until the following year" "so, what happened?" "we went up the pub and I beat the boys at pool," he smiles, "I mean with the skeleton?" "I don't know? all I know is that when we got back it was gone" "and Mr Broomfield?" "I knocked at his door and sometime later he came down and told us to get on with it" "when you were up the pub do you think Mr Broomfield had time to leave the property?" "nah, he didn't have time" "ok, Mr Carter you've been very helpful, thank you," Emily turns to leave, "hey if anyone else comes sniffing around, I don't know you and this conversation never happened; do you hear me?" "yes of course, Mr Carter," as Emily turns, she closes his gate and as she does, she glances at him one last time and he says, "I was sorry to hear about your dad", now making the connection, she had rather he hadn't mentioned that and she doesn't reply. By the time Emily had eventually got home her feet were sore, her arms were sore, and her head was sore having gone over and over this new information she had just been given and it looked like she made it home just in time as the weather looked like it was on the turn.

Emily on entering the cottage opens all the doors and puts away the groceries and as soon as she has, she makes a snack and heads for the garden and despite the now gathering storm clouds overhead she prefers this to the oppressively dark feeling she gets from within the house. Emily paces trying to put together the picture of these two young lovers Louis and Annie now pregnant, *their affair against the wishes of Louis's father the count*, Emily turns and strolls back towards the pond, *the count has Annie murdered on nothing more than trumped up chargers of being a witch and it was in this very pond!* Emily now startled looks back up to find that she is now stood directly in front of the smaller of the two old oak trees and her attention is drawn towards what she believes are some insects on the bark doing some sort of communication dance, weaving in and out around their queen, when suddenly this dance seems to intensify and in fact, comes bubbling out of the bark itself to form a new image, there comes a bolt of lightning that cracks the very air above her head and the bark transforms into a skeletal like face, eye's flaming, what flesh remained, hanging from cheek bones and forehead and the count snarled and hisses a foul stench at Emily, and she reels backwards, it felt like a combination of fear, shock and a paranormal power that did indeed propel her backwards with great force and speed and the next Emily knew she was plunging into water, cold numbing water that enveloped her, consumed her, and her pace slows, and her hearing dulls and for a brief moment the entire universe came to a complete stop as she hangs, suspended, frozen in time. As Emily stares up through the water and to the sky above there comes sight but not sound of another streak of lightening and the water around her begins to churn and swirl as she is forced onto her front, and through the bubbles and mist, an image begins to form and Emily having regained her composure and bearings now swims tentatively toward.

The shape shifts and the form crystallizes into the image of a girl sat in a heavy wooden chair, "ANNIE!" the name instantly floods into Emily's mind and she kicks frantically and pulls at the water to get to her, to save her. Emily eventually reaches her, and grabs hold of

Annie's forearms in an attempt to stop from floating away and the two young women are able to stare into each other's eyes and there comes a stillness, a moment of recognition and a small but sorrowful smile breaks out on the lips of Annie. Emily now claws at the brass buckle that holds Annie's right wrist and the new stiff leather put's up a fight and proves reluctant to let go of its prisoner, finally, it relents, and Emily is able to thread the strap through and bends it back using it as a leaver relieving the pressure just enough to allow her to pull the pin from the centre of the thick strap and the restraint now seem to just fall apart with ease. Emily now moves to Annie's left wrist with haste and begins the struggle once again when she feels Annie's hand wrap around hers and gently stops her attempt at her freedom, Emily looks up to see Annie's angelic, calm smiling face, strands of her golden hair flowed about her in slow motion and from Annie's lips she mouths the words "thank you, thank you, now go up," Emily, confused, froze not knowing quite what to make of this and Annie again mouths, "go up, Emily, go up" and this time she gestures with her head by nodding upwards. Emily is suddenly gripped with a feeling of complete sadness and the very real need for oxygen. Emily feels herself being dragged backwards through the dark mist and swirls and for a moment she becomes completely disorientated in the pitch darkness, she knows not what is up nor down until from above her comes the blinding white flash and although Emily can't hear a thing there is something deep within her, something primeval that tells her this is lightening, and lightening comes from above and she kicks and thrashes toward the source of where the light had come from.

She burst through the surface just in time to exhale what little air she had left in her lungs and gasps for oxygen and the need for air becomes all-consuming and she forgets to kick, she feels herself being dragged under again and she panics, forgetting all she had been taught when it came to water safety; she just wants out and she comes to the confused realisation that it's now turned to night and she can only just make out the sloped bank of the pond and she strikes out to reach it.

There comes a roll of thunder followed by the flash of lightening and she sees the bank more clearly and the outline of the house but try as she may her progress is slow and hampered as if something or someone is trying to stop her from getting out and a thought comes to her mind, *what if he is in here, what if he wants to drown me just like he did Annie*, and again Emily is gripped and almost frozen with fear and she screams, "HELP! HELP ME, PLEASE HELP!" the fear that something maybe lurking below these dark waters? and that something could be evil? could be the count? spurs Emily on and she finds a new strength, strength fuelled by sheer fear itself and she thrashes and kicks and soon her fingertips make contact with the bank of soil and she claws and drags at it but to no avail for as she attempts to lunge and pull herself up the more the bank seem to repel her and before long it becomes a slippery slope and Emily cry's and sobs at the futility of her struggle and again she is filled with the fear that something was slowly coming up from the depths to get her and as she looks over her shoulder, she again screams, "HELP! PLEASE, SOMEBODY HELP ME!" she thrusts out a hand and grabs a clump of wet soil and grass and from out of the dark her wrist is grabbed tightly and there comes a powerful force that propels her up the slippery slope and out in one foul swoop and she lands face down in grass, spluttering, expelling water and sucking in air and from out of the dark comes a voice, a voice she has never been happier to hear, "Emily, what on earth are you doing?" it was her mum; Sam. Sam bundles Emily up and slowly walks her toward the closest door, that of the conservatory and guides Emily in, Sam slips past her and she now frantically fumbles for the light switch, flips it on and Sam gasps in horror as she is startled backwards, for where her hands had been fumbling in the dark for the switch, there was now finger smears of dark red blood all over the wall, Sam turns and looks, wide eyed at her daughter who is one solid mass of congealing blood, her hair flat and matted to her head only the very white of her eyes giving away any sense of features and as large globules of blood drip from Emily and explode on the tiled floor about her feet, Sam screams.

Joe now franticly bangs on the kitchen door having found it to be locked and within a short while Sam out of breath having sprinted down from upstairs lets her in, "I came as quick as I could Sam, how is she" "I'm not sure? I've got her in the shower, can you help me with her clothes?" "sure, of course, Sam how did she try and do it?" "do what?" "try and take her life?" "she didn't, I mean, I don't know Joe, I'm just not sure of anything right now Joe," and Sam begins to cry, Joe puts an arm around Sam, "come on, let's get her sorted," Sam leads the way and Joe spots the phone on the island and its covered in blood and rounding the corner towards the stairs the tiled floor is also covered in blood, it looks like a novice had attempted ice skating in bloodied boots, again, climbing the stairs and more blood on the floor and bannister railing, "oh, my word Sam, what on earth has she done to herself?" Sam says nothing and the two walk into the bathroom to find Emily stood up in the shower clearly in a state of shock as she doesn't acknowledge either Sam or Joe as they try to speak to her, with blood everywhere the two women set about trying to peel the blood-soaked clothes from Emily's limbs and body. From down inside the house there comes a voice and with Joe's senses obviously heightened she grabs Sam arm, "there's someone in your house Sam," from below the voice comes again "Sam, Its Dr Hendricks", Joe now looks at Sam, "I called him shortly after you, YES WE'RE UP HERE DOCTOR," there comes the clatter of feet on the stairs and in through the door bursts the Doctor, he quickly assesses the situation and calmly takes charge, "good evening ladies if you could just step aside," and with a soft tone and deft touch he sets about examining Emily. Sam and Joe retreat and break out mops and cloths and have managed a pretty good clean up job and have made coffee when the Doctor comes back down bag in hand, "how is she Doctor?" asks Sam, "well, I've examined her from top to toe Sam and there's nothing? physical to report, however she hasn't said a word and she's in shock, I would advise that she goes to hospital, but I feel this would just add to the trauma, I've given her a heavy sedative which will simply knock her out but if you could keep an eye on her throughout the night, that would be good," Sam nods. "But what about all that blood Doctor?" asks Joe, "where did you say you found her again?" "she was in the pond", says Sam, "the pond?" says the Doctor with a frown on his face and a tone of unbelievability, he grabs the torch from beside the back door and all three now walk into the back garden and emerge from the mist beside the pond, the water now sits still and in the darkness, it appears solid and black and there are no conclusions to be made as they shuffle back in, making sure they're not bringing in anymore blood in on their shoe's, "well, that was inconclusive, however I've taken the precaution of retrieving a sample of the blood from Emily's clothes and I'll get that analysed at the lab and get back to you on that Sam" "thank you, Doctor," "ok well I'll bid you goodnight ladies and if there are any complications during the evening Sam call me will you," Sam thanks him again and he sees himself out of the kitchen door. "Thanks again Joe, I don't know what I'd do without you?" "think nothing of it Sam, you'd do the same for me, I know, and what I also know Sam is that I think we both could do with a bloody good stiff drink excuse the pun," and Sam smiles wearily.

Joe stay's with Sam and throughout the night they take turns to check in on Emily who seemingly slept soundly all night, Joe was of course as concerned as Sam, she had watched Emily over the years grow up to become a quite lovely young lady and if she'd had a girl herself she would have wanted her to be just like Emily, Emily in turn had over the years often referred to Joe as auntie Joe and it was with some relief for both as dawn broke that there hadn't been any more dramas for Emily but there was another reason that Sam couldn't wait for dawn to come and after checking once again on Emily she came downstairs and said to Joe, "right, let's you and I see just what's going on with this pond", the two step out into the garden and to the pond that sat glistening in the early morning light, dragonflies skimming the surface and the two stood and stared in dis-belief for although the water wasn't so clean that you could see the bottom, it was obvious that they were looking at just water and there wasn't a drop of blood to be seen anywhere even on the grass where Sam had dragged Emily to safety. "I don't understand Sam," says Joe and Sam without speaking turns and runs back into the house and up the stairs, Joe close on her heels. Although they had cleared up blood from floors and surfaces the night before Sam remembered that they had forgotten about Emily's clothes that they had left in the bottom of the bath, and what the Doctor had said about taking a sample of the blood from the clothes. Sam now bursts into the bathroom closely followed by Joe half expecting to find no clothes at all or to find clothes but just wet with water and not blood.

What hits Sam and Joe first is the pungent, acrid stench of putrefying blood and both have to cover their nose and mouths but it was the next intrusive invasions of their senses that truly made their flesh crawl, that of blue bottles, large slow-moving flies that if were not dive bombing them seemed intent on wanting to land and crawl on their skin and both squeal as they frantically try, all but in vain to swipe these Kamikaze creatures away. Sam wasn't quite sure whether she was glad, sad or frightened as she and Joe stared down into the bath to see Emily's clothes thick with congealed blood and now, they were confused, "this can't be right Sam, what on earth is going on?" Sam without turning away from this heaving pile, says, "Joe, do me a favour, go downstairs and bring me one of those thick bin liners and the marigolds please, you'll find them under the kitchen sink" "sure, ok" as Joe leaves Sam walks from the bathroom making sure she quickly closes the door behind her, and she steps to Emily's room and quietly opens her bedroom door and checks that Emily is still sleeping soundly, and Sam softly says out loud to herself, "you were right darling, there is something here." Joe returns with the bin liner and hands it to Sam, "what are you going to do Sam?" Sam dons the gloves and opens the black bin liner and begins shovelling in the heavily blooded clothes, "what are you going to do with them Sam, wash them?" "no Joe these are going straight out and, in the bin, I don't want them in this house" "ok, while you do that, I'll wash the bath out says Joe," Sam carries the really heavy bag down and out and struggles to lift and swing it into the wheel bin in the drive and as she closes the lid on this bloodied bundle she stops and looks back at the cottage with the feeling of uncertain dread and a feeling that something had gleefully watched her do this.

By the time Emily came around it was late, she estimated that it was perhaps mid-morning, it took a moment to register that someone was sat on the edge of the bed and as Emily squinted Sam slowly came into focus, "morning darling, how are you feeling?" "I'm ok", says Emily, "how about some breakfast?" "sure, that would be good" "tea, toast, and some cereal ok?" "that would be great actually," says Emily rubbing her eyes, "ok, in bed or downstairs?" "no, I'll come down, I need to move" "ok see you in a mo.," Sam leaves and Emily makes an attempt to sit up and she now becomes aware of just how much pain she is in; she had said to her mum that she was alright knowing full well that everything wasn't alright, but it was now trying to move that the full extent of her injuries became apparent, she was bruised, battered and sore from head to toe, everything hurt, and movement just exaggerated it for if she just moved a toe it had an effect on everything else over her entire body. She managed to sit up by rolling on her side and pushing her body up by her elbow and at the same time pushing the covers back and swinging her legs over the side of the bed and she groaned out a long exhale of pain that only stopped when she came to a rest. Emily sat for a moment and shallow panted like a woman in labour, *what the hell happened to me last night, she thought*, it felt like she had gone twelve rounds with the heavy weight champ of the world, she could feel with her tongue that not only were her teeth sore, they were loose. She reaches for her dressing gown that was at the end of the bed and again has trouble putting her arms behind her whilst trying to thread them into the sleeves, she looks down and there laid beside her bed is her journal, open, and there's writing, her writing but she could not for the life of her remember writing anything the night before, how could she? she was out cold, she knew the doctor had administered drugs he told her so, but there on the page was her writing. Emily picks up the journal with a struggle, places it on her knees and reads,

Emily's Light

As the mist rises over the bloody pond

The Owls sit quiet in their parliament song

Sit still the spirits of the night

Let the sun wield its lucid light

To warm the earth for to let me sleep

For tonight I have promises to keep

The blood runs from the pen and heals the paper of my soul

Owls guide the way of water and break the seal to unfold

Rise the twos

Snap the wood

For the source of darkness reaps no good

Join me tonight for life will spill the blood

Entice spirits, weave light for the love of the sister hood.

She closes the journal completely bewildered and somewhat curious that she hadn't even bothered to sign it and places it back on the floor. She steady's herself on the bedside cabinet and stands, very slowly and eventually comes to a not so upright position but that's the best it's going to get for now, she finds her flip flops without looking and shuffles like an old woman to the door. It takes Emily for ever to get downstairs, but she does not care this was about to be a long process of recovery and she knows it. Sam had prepared breakfast and on the island is a big bowl like cup of tea, a plate toast cut into triangles, marmalade on the side and a bowl of muesli, the good stuff, a small jug of milk, mums know how to make things feel better by just doing the little things and Emily slides gingerly onto the stool, picks up the tea, sips and sits with the cup just below her nose, steam filling the hood of her dressing gown and she becomes lost in a moment of contemplation and Sam wisely leave's her to it. Its only as Emily is finishing the last of the toast and marmalade that Sam joins her at the island, "how are you feeling now?" "much better, thanks" "do you remember much from last night?" and Sam is taken aback when Emily replies "everything" "I'm sorry Emily", "what for?" "for doubting you, disbelieving you when you were trying to tell me that something was here, and I'm sorry for that and I'm sorry for what has happened" "so you believe me now, that they're here" "yes Emily, I do and whatever 'they' are I'd quite like them to go back to where there from!" Sam leaves Emily to finish her breakfast and to go about some chores, she had cancelled all her appointments for that day, and she knew that Emily and she would talk more but when she was ready to do so. It took several days before Emily began to even feel like herself again and she spent most of her waking time in the garden, not wanting to be in the house, thinking, writing in her journal.

Sam had to go back to work for her masters, she was self-employed, but in name only. Emily had, to a fashion tried to reconnect with the outside world, a world that was still consumed, obviously with the pandemic, but things had begun to ease with the opening of shops and restaurants and there was a new sense of optimism as people gazed toward the night sky and a comet that had appeared from out of deep space and it proved a brief distraction before disappearing, as quickly as it came, supposedly behind the moon, to reappear apparently, some time in-around 6800 years into the future, and Emily wondered what life would be like then?

There had come a visit one evening by Dr Hendricks and an examination of Emily which showed she was on the mend, she had to lie when asked if she was still taking the drugs that he had prescribed for her and of course he left more which were not going to be taken but she felt it better not to say and to just go along with the rouse.

As Emily re-dressed in her bedroom, she overhears the conversation between the Dr and her mum now stood on the landing and she gathers that there must have been contact from the Dr to Sam at some point via phone over the previous few days for he had the vial of blood analysed and it had shown what it contains were indeed from ungulates, hooved animals such as cattle, pig and deer and not from a human source that had been feared. Sam had herself made inquiries with the local farming community for which she had come to know well, and it would seem no one had lost any animals of any sort that could have found their way into their pond and so, the whole thing remained a mystery, as for Emily, she felt a bit miffed that her mother and the Dr still felt it necessary to have such a conversation, and seemingly, behind her back. Emily, over the coming days, she began to regain her strength and thus begins to try and make some kind of sense of what's happening to her as she wanders from garden to house and back pausing to run through events in her head until she comes to the conclusion that she must put this information down as its starting to become over whelming.

Emily sits in the garden by the pond and opens her journal and she feel's that's its right to document these events here as this is where it all began, the pond and her finding her fathers present to her, the journal is where it must be documented and She thinks, pen in mouth, and then begins to scribble, first there came,

The green bottle that fell over!

The wet footprints on the landing going into the fireplace!

The bottle falling over again and pointing to the fireplace!

Emily quickly puts the journal down on the sun lounger and jumps up, "the fireplace!" she says and rushes through and into the living room and begins to examine the fireplace. It's a decent sized inglenook, you do have to bend your head to duck under the mantelpiece in which to get in but once there the area is quite spacious in that it goes back some four feet, which back in the day allowed the household to be able to place large logs on the grate and on either side there were small brick-built benches for people to be able to actually sit inside the fire on the nights when it got really cold. Emily now stands and stares upwards though the chimney and to where it emerges from the roof and the glimmer of blue sky. She follows the chimney back from the light into perpetual darkness and see's nothing other than the metal pegs hammered into the wall at intervals that small boys would use to climb when cleaning the chimney in a bygone age. Not sure what it is she is looking for, whether a mark, a sign, a loose brick? that conceals a scroll of parchment, anything but she has not a clue. Emily now crouches and examines the back wall of the fireplace and again other than the odd irregular brick, nothing, there's nothing to be seen, nothing she can feel that would all of a sudden be the piece to complete the puzzle. She ducks back out, turns and go's up the stairs over the landing and to the master bedroom and although this fireplace isn't as big, it doesn't have the interior seating, it's of a similar construction and in fact is older than the one downstairs.

Emily ducks in and under and stands for a while to allow her eyes to adjust to the dark, and again, from the open sky at the chimneys end she follows the shaft back again, there's the foot pegs and, "wait what's that?" about halfway up Emily thinks she sees something, an anomaly there on one side.

Emily's immediate knee jerk reaction is to climb to where this, whatever this was, to see, and then she stops herself and looks down, she's in flip flops, shorts and a hoodie, *not actually mountaineering gear*, she thinks, but then, *it's not that far to climb, and what could possibly go wrong*? Emily kicks off her flip flops and sensibly tests the first few metal pegs and they seem sound.

She takes a deep breath and places one hand on a peg just above head height and the opposite bare foot on a peg some three feet off the ground and she pulls and pushes simultaneously, she had done some climbing on a wall at college and the one piece of advice that she had taken away that day kept popping into her head, *three points of contact, three points of contact* and she strikes out for her goal seemingly not more than some ten feet away and as she climbs the chimney quickly closes in and becomes darker and oppressive as it seems to wrap itself around her. Emily can't remember when if ever in her lifetime this fire being lit, the one downstairs was regularly, particularly around Christmas but not this one and it soon becomes clear just how much soot had been left and generally how dirty it was. Emily is now checking every peg diligently before she will place her full weight on it and she is reaching out to the next when a wave of shock and fear races through her body and she withdraws her hand so quickly that she knocks her elbow and despite the pain she is fixated on what is sat looking at her with its large eight eyes.

Emily loved all creatures and would, have never killed anything but there were something's that she would rather not be close to and one was, and had always been, spiders and this particular one was big and black and had watched her climb all the way up to *it* and now *it* just sat there staring at her she could see what little light there was reflected in *its* black eyes, *it* wasn't about to move, *it* wasn't going anywhere. Emily groaned and gathered her composure and concluded that she would just have to brush *it* to one side and carry on, she was so close now.

Emily takes a sharp inhale of air and braces her back against the wall of the chimney as she reaches up and using the back of her hand go's to brush the spider to her right, she miss times her swipe and the spider had anticipated the move and instead of falling away harmlessly to one side, the spider falls, hits her in the forehead and then lands high up on her chest and she just able to make out its legs in her peripheral vision as she looks down, all hell breaks loose as Emily screeches out loud and flails about with her arms to try and knock it away and the next time she looks down the spider has gone, there comes a brief second of uncertainty laced with fear as she sits still and there comes the feeling that something is crawling on her bare foot, she cringes and screams all at once, over exaggerates her leg movement and franticly flaps her foot as though she is doing a front crawl swimming stroke, had it gone? she couldn't tell, Emily whimpers, something completely incoherent in the dark, she steels herself once more and slowly, tentatively she knows she has to move on. Emily reaches where she thought she'd seen the anomaly in the wall, and she brushes away the cobwebs and soot to reveal, nothing, there was nothing there, had it been an optical illusion all along? or perhaps it had been her mind, a wanting, a willingness to see something, anything.

The feelings of disappointment and failure takes over her and any fear's that she had of the darkness, dirt or spiders, no matter how big, now paled into insignificance and she leans her head forward onto her hand still gripping the peg in front of her and she sighs long and hard. From out of the darkness from over her right shoulder she hears the voice of a young female say in a low whisper into her ear, "I'm here", Emily's head is startled back into the upright position and she turns her head as to see someone stood behind her, but that's impossible, there was barely enough room for her inside the tight chimney and she was some ten feet off the ground, Emily says out loud to the wall beside her, "Annie, is that you?" there comes a pause and then the two pegs Emily is standing on instantaneously give way and again Emily screams as she is left dangling in mid-air in the confined, dirty spider infested chimney, she gathers her composure and bracing her bare feet against the cobweb covered walls and she is able to slowly lower herself back down to earth and to the safety of her mother's bedroom, and for the second time in recent days, Emily now finds herself showering once again fully clothed. *Back to the drawing board* thinks Emily as she trots downstairs and back out into the garden, and retrieves her journal and as she heads back up the stairs, she makes a note to self, to *let mum know there's a giant black spider loose in her room.*

Emily now sits crossed legged on the floorboards in front of the fireplace she had just descended covered in soot and webs, all the time keeping an eye out for her newfound friend. *Ok let's do this again*, she thinks, *but this time let's go about this logically and methodically*. She crosses out the lines she had written before and as a heading she writes, *what we know*.

What we know

Mr Aston recounts the story of Annie and Louis and how both die at the hands of the count. Chris Carter confirms he finds remains, presumably Annie's, and Broomfield supposedly Brings them into the house.

'Bang'

There comes from above Emily's head a low muffled almost inaudible thud and although it registers, Emily doesn't pay it much attention.

I end up in the pond and we come face to face Annie, and you told me to 'go up' so I would not be drowned,

'Bang'

There comes another thump and this time louder and Emily raises her gaze to the ceiling just above her, and out loud she says, "go *up*," "GO UP," she now shouts out with the sudden realisation, "Annie are you in the attic?" and there comes three heavy thuds and a small amount of soot falls from within the chimney and lands in front of Emily's legs. Emily jumps to her feet sending the journal flying, she heads out of her mum's room, turns the corner and steps towards the door at the bottom of the stairs that leads to the attic and the door is slammed in her face so violently that the draught from this makes her momentarily startled that she has to shut her eyes and jerk her head back. Emily grabs the handle and it won't budge; she places a foot against the bottom of the door and makes an attempt to shove it, but the door is solid, there is simply no movement.

Emily has taken to again pacing up and down but this time it's at the bottom of the garden, she now knows that's both Annie and the count can hear her voice, but she has become so paranoid over these last few months that now she wrongly or rightly suspects that they can read her mind. At what she hopes is enough of a distance from the house Emily begins to put together a plan, she now knows that the remains of Annie and that of her unborn child are somewhere in the attic, quite where she's not certain, but how many places could there be to hide bones? it was also obvious that the count is not and will not be happy with her removing the remains of Annie, particularly once he realises that she has decided that Annie's remains are to be taken to the cemetery and laid to rest alongside Louis in his grave, a decision that she had come to when she had asked herself where she would take Annie, and it seem the most plausible outcome, obvious really, *it's where she would want to go*, to be reunited with her lover Louis, even after three hundred and fifty years. There was something else that had struck Emily once again, as it had on many occasions just recently, the sudden and somewhat surprising loss of time, day and date, for the following day was the six of August the very day that Annie and Louis came to an end; all be it centuries before. She didn't know what it was, this thought, this feeling, this impulse or where it had come from, but she just knew that it must be this day that Annie is to be reunited with Louis. Emily finalizes her plot and diversionary tactics that's she hopes will buy her just enough time to get Annie out of the cottage before the count has any idea what's happening and as Emily strides back up towards the house, she feels pleased with her plan and then tries desperately to push it from her mind, all thought of great escape to come.

All that Remains

Emily wakes early but does not rise as she wants her mother to go off to work without her being a distraction and thus a delay to her leaving the house. Emily watches from behind her curtains as Sam reverses out of the drive and onto the lane and disappears out of sight. Emily, now in her dressing gown cleans her teeth and then tip toes downstairs, greets Mr D, flicks on the kettle, pulls down a mug and bowl, turns and heads to the cupboard under the stairs, opens the door and retrieves her father's rucksack and drop's it at the bottom of the stairs as she passes and continues to the kettle that's now is hissing and spluttering, and she slowly continues to make a cup of tea and thinks twice about the cereal as she just doesn't think her stomach can take it as it's now in knots. Emily turns with her tea and go's to head for the stairs pausing momentarily to pick up a wooden wedge that's usually used to prop open the kitchen door and the torch and puts these into the rucksack as she reaches it, she then sweeps up the rucksack places it over one shoulder and disappears up to her room. She checks to make sure the main body of the rucksack is empty and places the wedge on her bed, she now gets dressed but this time instead of her usual casual attire she dons t-shirt, jeans, hoodie and her stout walking boots, lacing them up properly to the very top so that they feel good and secure. Emily sips her tea, opens curtains and throws the duvet back over her bed and realises that she is just stalling and why? Because she is scared, Emily steadies herself, *come on you can do this*, she grabs the rucksack and places the wedge and torch in her pockets and on leaving her room she nonchalantly drops the rucksack by the door of the attic stairs as she passes and heads downstairs.

Emily go's directly to the room at the front of the cottage, the old courthouse, she drops the wedge at the bottom of the door and with her foot she slides it into position and pulls the door towards her to make sure that this now cannot be shut on her. Emily now stands in the centre of the room and waits for all to become still. She now says out loud, "count Bourbonne, I command you to come forth," there comes the sound of a low cruel chuckle from within the house, Emily shuffles nervously, "I command you count, come fourth, now!", and from above, Emily hears the sound of a door being slammed violently and again silence. "I know what you did to Annie Wright" there comes the rumble of a groan, she waits, and then says "I know what you did to your son, count", the whole house shakes so violently that Emily can hear dishes in the kitchen rattling and from above comes the sound of heavy foot fall running, and towards her! the stomps come down the steps, closer, and she turns to look down the hallway to see the count as he dismounts the stairs, but there is nothing, nothing there, and all stops and Emily gasps for air as she realises that she'd been holding her breath and she stares and stares but again, there's nothing there, but she knows he is there, looking at her.

There then comes the sound of boots on floorboards and nails clawing at walls as a force comes at Emily, a force so strong that it stops her from holding her ground and she is made to step backwards, the door is grabbed high up and there's an attempt to slam it, but the wedge does its job and the bottom of the door stays where it is, however, the top shatters and splinters as the hinge gives way. There's a heavy suppression that falls upon Emily, and she feels sick, nauseous, her head swims as she smells burning, the sickly-sweet scent of flesh on fire, she is suddenly gripped by the back of her hoodie and hurled through the air with such force that she crumples into a ball and is halfway down the hall before she makes contact with the floor but continues to slide at speed until she is well into the kitchen heading for the island. Emily rolls and springs to her feet and without hesitation clambers up the staircase using her hands as well as her feet, onto the landing and with one hand she grabs the handle of the attic door and with the other she scoops up the rucksack and with great relief the door gives, and she bursts through turns collapses on the stairs and kicks the door closed behind her and places her feet against this and braces herself for what she thought would be the inevitable impact of the count trying to force his way in, but nothing came, and all once again fell silent.

Emily sat and listened for some time trying desperately to catch any sound that would tell her where he was but there came no hints and after a while Emily came to the conclusion that he would have made an attempt to smash the door in by now and if he were behind her in the attic, he would now be attacking her from this side. She lifts her feet gingerly, one at a time from the door, trying desperately not to make a sound just in case the count is indeed, on the other side, the image of him, his ear pressed against the door, eyes closed, listening for her, a grin upon his cruel face popped into her head and a cold shiver ran through her soul. She stands and turns and tip toes up the narrow rickety wooden stairs and pops up from out of the floor like part of a magician's act, she retrieves the torch from her pocket, flicks it on and comes face to face with all the usual paraphernalia that people will discard into a loft, rugs, boxes, Christmas decorations, suitcases, tags still attached, a reminder of far flung destinations visited that right now did indeed seem a million miles away, beaches she wished she were sat on right now. She steps over the clutter of modern life and into the void beyond, that of the attic. The attic was vast, it covered the entire footprint of the cottage, one of the previous owners had the whole thing boarded out, and the roof pitch wasn't too shallow and a good proportion of this space you could walk about up right quite easily.

Emily looks to her left and see's the first of the two-chimney breast's and then to her right this was the chimney she wanted, the one she had fallen from, the one she had heard Annie's voice in. She moves towards this and becomes aware of hundreds of years of dust soot and of course, spider webs, and the whole time fearful of the door below crashing in at any moment.

She reaches the chimney and places her hands upon it, feeling for a recess or loose bricks, first one side and then the second and as she turns the next corner to the third, she is stopped, for the few weak rays of sunlight that have penetrated through the small web covered window at that gable end have illuminated two uneven courses of brick, about six in all.

Emily, now standing in front of these is just able to fit her fingertips in far enough on either side of the top brick and as she wiggles it from side to side it makes the rasping sound of brick on brick and once this key stone comes free the rest are easy going and she places them at her feet one by one to form a small pile on which she now stands and holding on to the wall with both hands Emily now peers into this black hole. Although the attic is dark the hole is darker, and it takes a little while for Emily's eyes to focus on what lays within. There in the dim light she spies a hessian sack, she gently reaches in and picks it up by the neck and is surprised at just how light it feels. Emily steps down from her plinth and carefully places the bag on the floor, she rolls back the neck and shines the torch in. Emily goes from kneeling to slumping to her bum as the torch illuminates from the dark a pile of white bones and Emily finds it difficult to make the connection between these and the beautiful young woman that she had seen in the courthouse and the pond and her heart sinks further as she sees the tiny skull of what was Annie's child and it all becomes too much for Emily and she sobs uncontrollably, "I'm so sorry Annie," she mutters in the dark as large bomb like tears fall and thud into the bone-dry old oak floorboards scattering centuries of dust in all directions.

Emily gathers herself and unshoulders the rucksack and with the reverence they deserve she carefully places Annie and child inside and makes sure its secure before putting the rucksack back on. She stands, sniffs, wipes her face, turns and heads back towards the stairs, she steps over the family junk, puts the torch between her teeth and bracing herself with her hands on either side of the walls she attempts to lower herself down the stairs one step at a time, trying desperately not to make a single sound, even with her breathing so much so that by the time she reaches the bottom she has made herself short of breath and she must pause for a while in which to regain it for she knows not what to expect on the other side of that door and she has to be ready.

Emily turns off the torch and winces when it makes a small clicking sound as she does, she pauses and listens as she continues to put it in her pocket. Emily now, oh so gently wraps her fingers around the door handle, leans forward and places her ear against the door, closes her eyes and strains to hear anything she can from the other side, and there comes again the image to her mind of the count doing the same thing, only a half inch of wood separating her from his evil world and again, a shiver runs cold within her. She takes a deep, slow, silent breath, stills herself and turns the door handle to the left and she feels the pressure being released on the door as the lock disengages, she pushes upon the door, half expecting there to be no give and that her premonition to be true, that of the count holding them captive, but no, the door gives and there comes the feelings of relief and safety that early morning light does often bring, as it floods in and warmly wraps itself around her.

Emily opens the door wide enough to put her head through and she scans the entire landing, there's nothing, there's no one, she slowly pushes the door wide and leaves it there not wanting to make any further noise by closing it, she steps warily to the top of the staircase and stops, she listens and sniffs the air, there's no smell of burning and she looks over the railings and down onto the hallway below and again, all's quiet. Emily now takes one step at a time, constantly looking to her left and right and occasionally over her shoulder to where she had just come, halfway down she pauses and looks over the railing once more and this time she is able to see down the hall and into the old courtroom and again nothing is moving, she looks in the direction of the kitchen and it's right there just a few feet away and she is almost overcome with the joy at the statement, *I've made it,* but she holds herself back for a moment and resist the urge to *go for it,* and thinks, *ok, so there's about six steps, two yards to the kitchen, two yards to the door and of course the door will be locked and we're out and onto the lane, ok here go's.*

Emily leaps from the stairs and abandoning all attempts of remaining stealthy hits the hallway floor and using that momentum instantly moves forward and into the kitchen, turns right, skidding on floor tiles, hands outstretched one for the door handle, one for the key, BOOOOM, out from her right comes a wave of force so fast and powerful it takes Emily clean of her feet and propels her over the island and she comes to a crashing halt as she makes contact with the cooker front, thankfully she had landed on her side and not her back which would have caused damage to Annie, however the initial hit or her hitting the stone floor had knocked the wind out of her and all she can do right now is to sit up, raise her knees and with her head hung, try's as she may to suck air in.

From the other side of the island and beyond her vision come's the sound of someone slowly stepping towards her, dragging one foot as it comes, and from around the corner comes first a leather buckled boot that comes high up on the leg of its wearer, a leather trouser leg is tucked into this, the other leg follows, being dragged, no boot, most of the flesh gone, what remains just hangs from exposed bone that makes a tapping sound as it touches the tiled floor, Emily, dazed tilts her head back and her eyes go wide at the vision before her, from a thick leather belt comes a billowing white blouse, torn in tatters and protruding from this are burnt limbs again a combination of bone and flesh, but it was the face that struct the most terror into Emily for there was little hair, no nose, the flesh around the eyes had been completely burnt away leaving two glaring none moving eyes, dead and still, the only movement was a flicker of flame in each, it's lips and cheeks were also gone, exposing a full set of teeth that looked as though they were constantly snarling, *it* stops, and *it* places one hand on the wooden countertop that instantly begins to smoulder and *it* glares and grimly smiles down upon Emily, the count has returned.

The count reaches forward his nails are so long they make his hands look claw like and he grabs hold of one of the straps to Emily's rucksack and launches her back over the island with ease, again Emily collapses in a crumpled heap in the hall, this time was just as painful as the first.

Emily raises up, supported on her arms behind her and she notices the strap the count had grabbed hold of was now smouldering and half melted, as she sits and stares back down the hall the count rounds the corner from the kitchen, and they lock eyes, "you will die now witch," the count growls and as he moves towards her. Emily begins to move in a crab like fashion backward fast into the courtroom and is now sat in the centre of the room as the count steps in and as soon as his bony foot touches the carpet it instantly begins to smoulder. He lunges at Emily, she falls onto her back lifts her legs and kicks with all her might directly into the counts ribs and there comes the sound similar to a bundle of dry sticks being snapped, but the count doesn't move either backwards or with pain, he simply glares at Emily, his jaw drops open and he laughs at her, a laugh that mocks her, that tells her she is done for and Emily can see the exposed muscles and sinew now tightening in readiness to strike again and it's all that Emily can do is wince and cower with anticipation of the imminent flurry of blows that are about to rain fire down upon her.

From out of nowhere Mr Darcy leaps onto the back of the counts head and there comes a blurred flurry of claws swiping wildly at the counts eyes, the count reels backwards writhing in shock from the sudden attack and he roars with anger as he tries to strike Mr D away but to no avail as Mr D has every intent to harm and Emily's not sure what now frightens her most the sight of the count or the high shrill screeches coming from Mr D, Emily wastes no time and gets to her feet, picks up a foot stool and throws it at the front window and without any thought of cutting herself she now scrambles through this just as the room begins to fill with smoke. Emily falls onto the front drive, rolls, jumps to her feet, looks back through the smog just in time to see Mr D disappear back down the hall at speed, Emily doesn't stop long enough to see where the count is at, she just turns and sprints into the lane and up the hill towards the graveyard, she glances back only once to see smoke now billowing from the broken window.

Emily makes the five hundred yards to the junction before she has to stop to catch her breath, doubled in two with a stitch to her side she mutters, "come on, you can do this."

The count leaves the smouldering smoke filled room, walks back down the hall, turns left into the kitchen and smashes through the rear door, what remains is left splintered and hanging from its hinges and the count strides past the pond and down the garden toward the second body of water and disappears into the dense foliage. He locates an area on the floor that's covered with years of fallen leaves, he drops to his knees and begins to sweep these away and as he does some of the dryer more brittle leaves catch and begin to crackle into life with flame, he stops as he sees his goal, the edge of a large flat stone which he wraps his fingers around one edge and with the rasping sound of stone on stone he effortlessly slides this back to reveal a dark deep void dropping away into the earth, he wastes no time and drops into the hole, a plume of smoke, much like a cloak following him into the darkness.

Emily makes it just past the pub before she has to stop and rest again, and she can't believe just how unfit she has become in only four months of lockdown, "ok, not far now," she says, and her mind now turns to the task of how she will in fact get Annie's remains into Louis's grave, *perhaps she'll be able to find a shovel*, she thinks.

The count is now surrounded in complete darkness, but it has no effect on him for he knows these tunnels well, they have come to be over the centuries his only means of breaking free from the curse of capture that has held him prisoner within the beams of willow cottage. He runs head long into the dark clawing at the walls as he goes. Soon the count reaches his destination and there above his head now sits a large slab of stone that he had located and excavated some time before and he pushes against it and it gives, and as light pours into the tunnel the count slides the large heavy slab to one side with ease.

With one bound the count is now squat, hunched over as he surveys the dim lit room that he is now in and he see's barrels that are silver and pipes and machinery and he looks up to see wooden boards and the underside of a floor and without hesitation he springs upward with such a loud and explosive force that he smashes clean through the floor and planks are splintered in all directions about this room.

The count is now stood in a cloud of smoke and debris in the middle of the bar of the Fox and Hounds pub, his eyes searching for what he has come for, and there he spies it, for hanging above the bar is his precious sword. He pulls it down and briefly pauses for a moment as he looks at it lovingly, he turns to see sat in the corner frozen to his seat, leaning on his walking stick an old regular of the pub who had dropped in for his usual daily pint, the count says nothing, and neither can the old gent, such is his shock at this vision, the count steps and drops down through the floors and back into the tunnel.

The skies darken as a mighty storm rapidly rolls in overhead and in the garden of the courthouse a black cloaked, hooded figure appears by the pond and steps before the old, gnarled oak tree.

Emily reaches the gate way of the graveyard and she pauses for a moment, both hand on top of the gate and allows herself a small, brief congratulative smile, "made it, Annie," she says and as she is saying the final syllables there comes a blow to her lower back so strong that it violently pitches her clean over the gate and once again Emily finds herself sliding along a gravel path and this time she is almost up ended onto her face, "no, not again," she whimpers and suddenly the pain still in her back from what was obviously a kick has now intensified and she realises that her clothes are on fire, she rolls to extinguish the flames and the pain and heat soars to near unbearable.

Medea pulls down the hood of her cloak and places her hands upon the sacred oak and begins her incantation, the spell to send this monster once and for all to hell. From her hands a light does shine and penetrates the bark and vein like lines come to life and begin to glow and grow down towards its very roots and beyond.

The count kicks the gate sending it off its hinges and steps onto hallowed ground and not taking his eyes from Emily for a moment he hobbles on skeletal foot towards her and as he comes he unsheathes the sword with a zing, as though the blade itself does sing with joy, for after all these years it's too taste blood once more.

The storm rages and crashes overhead as lightening illuminates and exaggerates the features of the counts grizzly face when beside the entrance of the graveyard a tall oak that stands guard begins to shiver, a light grows up from beneath the ground and moves within its bark to give the impression of back lit fish scales, the ground rumbles beneath them and rises up some two feet before the pressure becomes too much and the ground cracks and opens up to reveal thick tree roots that shoot out like the tentacles of some manically possessed octopus, they seek out knowingly and find the count and squirm their way up and around his legs and weave in and out of his rib cage and grab hold of his face having first come up through his jaw and gripping hold of him firmly like a giant hand they rip him down and through the cracks at speed breaking all and any bones that try to give any resistance, his sword is sent clattering to one side as a fountain of black blood is sent cascading into the air as the count is pulled beneath the earth his hand clawing at the sky the last of him to be seen and the light go's, cracks close and the earth subsides and levels as quickly as it had risen, a roll of thunder announcing the departure of the count and all becomes still.

Medea straightens and takes her hand from the oak, satisfied that her work, for now, has finally been done and she heaves a sigh of relief.

Emily still sat on the floor staring in disbelief, she dare not move, dare not breathe in case the thing from beneath, whatever that was hasn't done what it clearly intended to do and at any moment the count will burst back through and go to attack her again. After what seems like an age Emily draws her legs up and under her and pushing off the ground and with a great deal of discomfort, she finally manages to raise herself up first one leg then the next. As Emily stands, she feels dizzy with pain, she takes a breath to try and straighten herself and looks about, there to her right is Louis's grave and as she takes the rucksack off, she limps towards it; she drops to her knees and places her hands on the grass of his grave wondering how's she's to break through. Emily now stands again with purpose and leaving the rucksack by the grave she hobbles over to where the count's sword lays, picks it up and is surprised at just how heavy it feels and heads back to the grave. With both hands holding the blade halfway down Emily now digs at the soil and a thought comes over her of just how ironic this was that the very sword that sent Louis to his grave was now the very same that will reunite him with his love, Annie.

The soil did not give much resistance and before long Emily is more than two feet down and a trench some two feet long or more and she stops sits back up and reaches for the rucksack pulls the hessian sack out and places it beside the grave. Emily now very carefully removes each of Annie's bones and as best she can, places them into the ground in the right configuration, the last thing to go in is the remains of the child which she places at Annie's tummy.

Emily wasn't about to say a prayer, frankly she didn't know how but she did say a few words, "Annie, you are finally at home now, with Louis, be at rest, rest easy now my friend" with both hands she pushes the soil back over and covers Annie, she stands with the aid of the sword, bends to retrieve the rucksack when there comes a blinding flash of light that Emily initially thinks is ball lightning, but it did come from in front of her and she is startled backwards and as the light grows and intensifies to engulf the entire grave and Emily is filled with a sense of peace, a warmth as opposed to a feeling of dark and dread that she had come accustomed to of late, and there forms before her two figures, one of which she recognises instantly, that of Annie and the other must be of Louis, in each other's arms, smiling at Emily and bathed in this warm light she smile's back.

Annie breaks from Louis and moves towards Emily and she is taken back when Annie says to her quite clearly, "thank you Emily, for all you have done," Emily again smiles and nods in recognition as Annie looks to one side as if listening to someone and says, "he wants you to be happy Emily," Emily now startled says, "who Annie?" "your father," she replies, "but why did he not come himself" "for he allowed me to come instead, Emily," Annie smiles and raises one hand in goodbye and the light begins to fade and finally closes and Emily is surprised at just how dark it has become about her.

Emily leaves the graveyard satisfied that her work is done and hobbles off back down the lane, the counts sword in hand and Emily is struck with the thoughts and feelings that reflection will bring, for these past few months had indeed been weird to say the least. *Had the lose of her father and the subsequent out pouring of grieve brought forth the spirits of Annie and that of the count and were her actions of helping Annie get back to her love a way of coping or coming to terms, she could not for now, begin to fathom the complexities of the situation, she was that exhausted, and glad to know of her fathers presences, but one thing kept coming back to her and that was the feeling that she had been tested, but by who?*

Halfway down back down the lane and Emily is jolted back to the here and now, for she spies something that's sat just inside a hedge row, the unmistakable fluffy ball of Mr Darcy and she sweeps him up and holds him in her arms, "extra big bowl of food for you tonight my brave man," and although some of his fur has been scorched he's the same old none fussed saggy cat as before and Emily loves him even more.

As Emily turns the corner into the drive, she is met by the neighbours from what was the brewery back in the day and they rush to her with concern, she had forgotten how she had left the cottage, "are you ok?" and where's your mum Emily?" she assured them she was fine and that mum was at work and they re-assured her that despite the door being smashed from its hinges and a small fire in the front room that they had successfully put out, things were, relatively all ok considering, and they went on to ask, what had happened? "you wouldn't believe me if I told you" she replies with a smile.

Way off in the distance upon a hilltop stood beneath a willow tree, Medea pulls down the hood of her cape and gazing towards the horizon to the east says, "and so…… it begins."

The End

Inspired by true events.

Owlsden Witches Key ©

Further Works to come by the Author

A Boy from the Valleys published 2020.

The Owlsden witches 2, To pay the piper, estimated release date early 2021.

The Owlsden Witches 3, The final dance, estimated release date late 2021.

Contacts

www.LGM McAvoy author.com

Leon McAvoy author Face book.

Leon McAvoy Instagram.

Leon McAvoy Twitter.

Leon McAvoy LinkedIn.